"My only alternative is to find myself a wife...and where am I going to find someone who'd be prepared to take me on with a baby?"

Ellie looked at Jack with a peculiar mixture of pain and pleasure.

It was wonderful just to be near him.

She drew a deep breath. "What about here?" she asked before she had a chance to lose her nerve.

"Here?" Jack's expression was half abstracted, half puzzled, clearly wondering if he had understood her properly.

"You could marry me," Ellie heard her voice saying.

D0615670

OUTBACK
Brides

In the hot, dusty Australian Outback,
the last thing a woman expects to find is a husband....

Clare, the Englishwoman, Ellie, the tomboy
and Lizzy, the career girl, don't come to this harsh,
beautiful land looking for love.

Yet they all find themselves saying "I do"
to a handsome Australian man of their dreams!

In January
Baby at Bushman's Creek

In March
Wedding at Waverley Creek

In May
A Bride for Barra Creek

Welcome to an exciting new trilogy by rising star
Jessica Hart

Celebrate three unexpected weddings, Australian-style!

WEDDING AT WAVERLEY CREEK

Jessica Hart

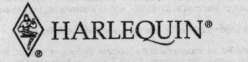

TORONTO • NEW YORK • LONDON
AMSTERDAM • PARIS • SYDNEY • HAMBURG
STOCKHOLM • ATHENS • TOKYO • MILAN • MADRID
PRAGUE • WARSAW • BUDAPEST • AUCKLAND

ISBN 0-373-03646-9

WEDDING AT WAVERLEY CREEK

First North American Publication 2001.

Copyright © 2000 by Jessica Hart.

All rights reserved. Except for use in any review, the reproduction or utilization of this work in whole or in part in any form by any electronic, mechanical or other means, now known or hereafter invented, including xerography, photocopying and recording, or in any information storage or retrieval system, is forbidden without the written permission of the publisher, Harlequin Enterprises Limited, 225 Duncan Mill Road, Don Mills, Ontario, Canada M3B 3K9.

All characters in this book have no existence outside the imagination of the author and have no relation whatsoever to anyone bearing the same name or names. They are not even distantly inspired by any individual known or unknown to the author, and all incidents are pure invention.

This edition published by arrangement with Harlequin Books S.A.

® and TM are trademarks of the publisher. Trademarks indicated with ® are registered in the United States Patent and Trademark Office, the Canadian Trade Marks Office and in other countries.

Visit us at www.eHarlequin.com

Printed in U.S.A.

CHAPTER ONE

ELLIE parked the ute in the shade of the gum tree and got out. She was stiff after the long drive, and she paused for a moment with her hand on the door, her eyes on the homestead before her.

Bushman's Creek. Jack's home.

It was over three years since she had seen him, but his image shimmered in the heat as clearly as if he stood before her as he had then, vibrant with reckless energy, smiling that smile that made the breath clog in her throat, brown eyes alight with laughter.

Ellie sighed. She had tried so hard to forget Jack. She had reminded herself a million times that Jack was simply an old friend, someone who thought of her—if he thought of her at all—as no more than the kid sister he had never had.

She had tortured herself by remembering every one of his girlfriends, all of whom had been pretty and lively and about as different from her as they could possibly be. She had even stayed away for three long years in the hope that his memory would fade, but none of it had done any good. All she had wanted was to see him again.

And now she was back.

She had thought it would be safe enough. Jack, her mother had said vaguely, was away. No risk of running into him and getting sucked back into that cycle of hopeless longing. Ellie remembered the confidence with which she had set off that morning, and smiled wryly to herself. She should have known better. Jack might not be here, but the memory of him lurked wherever she looked, almost as disturbing and exciting as Jack himself.

Making a determined effort to push his image aside, Ellie banged the door shut with unnecessary force and headed across the dusty yard to the homestead. She wasn't here because of Jack. She was here to find out exactly what her wayward elder sister was doing, and why she was staying with Jack's brother, Gray.

'Ellie!' Far from seeming guilty or defensive, as Ellie had half expected, Lizzy was delighted to see her. 'I can't tell you how much I've been longing for someone to gossip with,' she confided when the excitement of their first meeting for three years was over and they were sitting at the worn kitchen table. 'It's been so *boring* with no one to talk to all day.'

At least that gave Ellie the opening she needed. 'Lizzy, what are you doing here?' she asked. 'Mum told me you'd broken off your engagement and moved in with Gray...what on earth's going on?'

'Oh, trust Mum to get the wrong end of the stick!' Lizzy rolled her eyes. 'I *have* broken off my engagement, but of course I haven't moved in with Gray! We decided we weren't suited a long time ago. No, I'm just holding the fort until Clare gets back.'

'Clare? Who's Clare?'

'Gray's wife. Didn't Mum tell you about the wedding?'

Ellie shook her head in confusion. 'Do you think you could start again at the beginning?'

'It's perfectly simple.' Lizzy poured boiling water into the teapot and turned to set it on the table. 'Gray married an English girl called Clare a couple of months ago. I wish you could have been here, Ellie. It was a lovely wedding.'

She sighed nostalgically as she pulled out a chair and sat down. 'They're in England at the moment, having a long-overdue honeymoon. I was at a loose end anyway, and it suited me to get away from Perth for a while and help out here,' she explained as she poured the tea into two mugs. 'But I'll be hot-footing it home as soon as they get back, so you can tell Mum to stop worrying!'

Ellie took the mug her sister held out automatically. 'Gray's not here?' she said, as if she had only just realised what Lizzy had said. 'Do you mean you're here on your own?'

'Oh, no,' said Lizzy casually. 'Jack's here.'

Ellie's heart jerked painfully, the way it always did whenever Jack's name was mentioned, and she put the mug down with a hand that was not quite steady.

'Jack?' she said, horribly conscious of the tight, high note in her voice. What was it about the mere thought of Jack that made it hard to breathe normally? She cleared her throat. 'I thought Mum said that he was away.'

'He was. He travelled around the States and South America for a while, but he came home about a month ago. I'm surprised Mum hasn't heard.'

Ellie didn't reply. Green eyes oddly unfocused, she was gazing out of the window. Beyond the verandah, the great ghost gums hung over the creek, their branches outlined in crystalline detail against the blue glare of the outback sky, but Ellie didn't see them. Jack's face shimmered in front of her eyes, and all at once she was intensely conscious of the wooden chair beneath her thighs, of the colour of the mug and the smell of the tea and the beat of her own heart.

Jack. The world was more vivid just knowing that he was near.

'How...how is he?' she asked, trying desperately to sound casual.

'Well...' Lizzy hesitated, and at the sound of steps outside an expression that was almost relief flitted across her face. 'You can see for yourself,' she said. 'This'll be Jack now.'

There was a clatter as the screen door leading out to the verandah banged shut, and without quite realising what she was doing Ellie rose to her feet, clutching the back of her chair for support as she faced the door.

Jack was brushing the dust off his hat as he came into the kitchen. 'Lizzy, have you—' He broke off as he realised that Lizzy wasn't alone, and looked enquiringly.

Every time Ellie prayed that the magic would be broken, and every time it was the same. All Jack had to do was walk into the room and the air evaporated from her lungs, leaving her breathless and giddy and intensely conscious of the blood singing along her veins.

Every time she prayed that he would be less attractive than she had remembered, but he never was. He was always exactly the same. The same long, lean body, the same dark blond hair, the same brown eyes starred with laughter lines. The same puzzled look as he searched his memory for why she looked vaguely familiar.

He hadn't carried *her* image in his heart since they had last met, Ellie thought sadly. She was used to not being remembered. It wasn't that she was plain. She was just unremarkable, just ordinary. Ordinary brown hair, ordinary eyes, a quiet, ordinary face.

'Hello, Jack.'

Her fingers dug into the back of the chair, she forced herself to sound casual. It was always like this, pretending to be politely pleased to be meeting an old friend, terrified that someone would guess how she felt. Sometimes Ellie marvelled that no one ever had. Couldn't they all *see* what he did to her just by standing there? Couldn't they hear her heart thudding against her ribs?

Jack's face cleared in belated recognition. 'Ellie!' he said, smiling as he gave her a brotherly hug. 'I didn't recognise you there for a moment. You've grown up!'

She had grown up a long time ago, but Jack hadn't noticed. He would always be vaguely surprised to discover that she wasn't still running around in dungarees with her hair in bunches, Ellie thought with an edge of bitterness. She would only ever be Lizzy's little sister, too young to play, too young to dance, too young to kiss.

'It's good to see you again,' he went on with a final squeeze of her shoulders. 'I haven't seen you for ages.'

'Three and a half years,' said Ellie, then cursed herself for sounding as if she had been keeping count. 'About,' she added lamely. Her knees felt weak from his touch, and she sank back down onto her chair.

Jack laid his hat on the table, and it seemed to Ellie that a faint shadow crossed his face. 'What have you been doing with yourself all that time?' he asked.

Loving you. Trying to forget you. 'Oh, you know… working, travelling, that kind of thing.'

She watched him covertly as he pulled out a chair and sat down opposite, and saw with something of a shock that he wasn't quite the same after all. For the first time since she had known him, he looked tired. The vibrant, restless energy had gone. There was a strained look now in the eyes that had used to glint with daredevil charm, and the long, curling mouth had hardened into a bleak line.

A cold feeling settled in the pit of Ellie's stomach as she looked at him. What's happened? she wanted to cry, but Jack was forcing a smile, asking her where she had been travelling.

'In the States, mostly,' she said, still distracted by the change in Jack's expression. 'I was a nanny for a bit, and then I got a job on a ranch in Wyoming. I loved it there.'

'I don't know why you didn't just stay at home,' commented Lizzy, eyeing her younger sister with resigned affection. 'I can't believe that you spent three years in the States and didn't go to New York once!'

'I don't like cities.' Ellie wondered why she always felt so defensive about it. 'I'm not like you, Lizzy. I'm a country girl.'

'There's nothing wrong with that,' said Jack, smiling slightly as he looked from one sister to the other.

It was hard to believe that they were related. Lizzy was blond and bubbly with bright blue eyes and an indefinable air of style, overshadowing, as always, her quiet sister. Both girls wore jeans, but there the resemblance ended. Lizzy's jeans were beautifully cut, and she wore with them a fine white shirt more suitable to shopping or a casual alfresco lunch than an outback cattle station.

Ellie, on the other hand, looked ready to help out down at the cattle yards. Her jeans were serviceable, the blue shirt worn with use, and the hair waving softly around her face had been cut to demand as little attention as possible.

Aware of how dull she always appeared compared to vibrant Lizzy, Ellie hurried to change the subject.

'Lizzy's been telling me that Gray's married,' she said a little breathlessly. 'I'm sorry I missed the wedding.'

'So am I,' said Jack, and she looked at him in surprise. She couldn't imagine Jack not being at his own brother's wedding.

'You weren't here?'

He shook his head.

'Why, what were you doing?'

There was an odd little pause. Jack glanced at Lizzy, then opened his mouth to speak, but before he could answer a crackle broke the suddenly tense silence, followed, incredibly, by the sound of babbling.

Ellie, who had just lifted her mug, froze with it halfway to her lips and stared around her in puzzlement. It was so unlikely a sound to hear in the bachelors' kitchen at Bushman's Creek that she couldn't help wondering if she had imagined it. 'Did you hear that?' she asked hesitantly. 'It sounded almost like a baby!'

Lizzy and Jack grinned. 'It is a baby,' said Lizzy, pointing at a baby alarm plugged in on the worktop to show where the noise was coming from. 'That's Alice.'

Ellie put down the mug so abruptly that tea slopped over onto the table, but she didn't notice. She was staring at her sister as all sorts of wild possibilities chased themselves through her mind. 'You've got a *baby*?' she said, very carefully, and Lizzy laughed at her expression.

'Don't worry, she's not mine—although I wish she was! She's so gorgeous!'

'You don't say that when you're trying to feed her,' said Jack, and even in the midst of her amazement Ellie couldn't help the familiar twist of envy as she saw the affectionate look that passed between him and her sister. Lizzy and Jack were the same age, and they had always been very good friends.

'Where did this baby come from?' she asked blankly. 'Surely she's not Gray's?'

She was looking at Lizzy, who was shaking her head, and so was quite unprepared for what came next.

'She's mine,' said Jack.

A clock somewhere ticked into the long, long silence

that followed. Very slowly, Ellie's eyes moved from her sister to Jack.

He didn't say what I thought he said, she told herself frantically. He's joking. Staring at him, green eyes dark and blank with shock, she willed his face to break into a teasing grin, hoping against hope that he would laugh and tell her that of course he wasn't serious, of course he didn't have a baby.

Having a baby would mean that he had found someone he truly loved and had settled down, and why would he do that? He was careless, carefree Jack, who always had a different girl in tow, who had always enjoyed life far too much to saddle himself with the responsibility of a wife and child.

No! she wanted to shout. Tell me it's not true!

But Jack only looked back at her with a twisted smile. 'It was a surprise to me, too,' he said.

It was the news Ellie had dreaded as long as she had known that she was in love with Jack. She hadn't been able to do anything about the fact that he didn't love her, but loving him had been bearable because his affairs were never serious, because it had been obvious that Jack simply wasn't the type to settle down.

Except that now he had.

Ellie felt as if an iron hand had gripped her round her throat, and she was submerged in a great, rolling wave of despair mingled with sheer rage at her own stupidity. How many times had she let herself believe that Jack would never commit himself to one woman? All those nights, all those *years* wasted, dreaming that he would look at her one day and the scales would fall from his eyes, that he would realise then that she was the only woman he could ever truly love!

How could she have pinned so many hopes on such a

fantasy? Of *course* Jack was going to find someone special in the end. Of course it wasn't going to be her.

Jack and Lizzy were both looking at her expectantly. She had to say something, but her tongue was so unwieldy in her mouth that she had trouble getting the words out. 'I...didn't realise...you were...married, too,' she managed at last. Her voice sounded as if it was coming from a long way away.

Sadness flickered across Jack's face. 'I'm not.'

'But...' Totally confused by now, Ellie looked dumbly at the baby alarm, which was still emitting the sound of incomprehensible baby conversation. Had she misheard after all?

Lizzy put a hand on Jack's arm. 'Do you want me to explain?' she asked gently.

'No, it's all right.' Jack mustered a reassuring smile. 'I'll do it. I'm going to have to get used to telling people how I suddenly acquired a daughter.'

Turning back to Ellie, he drew a deep breath. 'Pippa—Alice's mother—came to Bushman's Creek as a cook, nearly two years ago now. She was an English girl, travelling around Australia, but as soon as she arrived it was as if she'd always belonged here. I fell in love with her the moment I laid eyes on her.

'She was...' Jack's voice cracked slightly, and he paused for a moment. 'She was the kind of person who lights up a room when they walk into it,' he went on at last.

Like you, thought Ellie.

'I'd never felt like that about anybody before,' said Jack, unaware of her mental interruption. 'I suddenly realised what love was all about. It was the same for Pippa. We had three wonderful months together, and then...'

Ellie swallowed. 'Then what?'

'Then we blew it.' Jack smiled tiredly. 'We had one of those stupid little arguments about nothing, and somehow it got out of control. Before either of us quite knew what had happened Pippa had packed her bags and gone back to England, saying she never wanted to see me again.'

He sighed, and although he looked at Ellie it was obvious that he was seeing the girl he had loved and lost. 'I should have stopped her getting on that plane, but I was too angry, and too pig-headed, and too bloody *stupid* to go after her straight away,' he said with sudden bitterness. 'I told myself Pippa was too emotional and dramatic for the outback, and that I'd soon get over her.

'The only trouble was that I didn't. I spent a year missing her and pretending that I wasn't. I tried everything I could to forget her, but nothing worked. There were memories of her wherever I looked, and in the end I thought it would be easier if I went away for a while. I spent a little while in the States, and then went on to South America. I thought that would be a place where there would be no associations to remind me of Pippa, but it was no good, and in the end I just gave up.'

The way she had done, thought Ellie, remembering her own desperate attempts to dislodge Jack from her mind. She understood more than he realised. She knew exactly what it was like to realise that there was no point in struggling any longer and that she might as well accept that Jack was the only man she was ever going to love.

'I got on a plane to London,' he told her, his voice slowing as he reached the most painful part of his story. 'I knew I could contact Pippa through her sister, so I went there first. I'd planned exactly what I was going to say. I was going to tell Pippa just how much I loved her.

I was going to beg her to marry me and come back to Bushman's Creek. I was going to promise to make her happy.'

Ellie listened numbly. Every word was like another layer of ice closing around her heart. She wanted to close her eyes and cover her ears, but she couldn't look away from the anguish in Jack's expression as he stopped to draw a steadying breath.

'I was too late,' he said, his voice empty of all expression. 'When I finally got to Clare's flat, there was no one there.' He looked away, his gaze resting blindly on the kettle, a muscle working in his jaw the only clue to the suppressed emotion inside him. 'A neighbour told me that Pippa had died not long after her baby had been born, and that her sister had taken the baby to be with its father in Australia.'

'Oh, Jack…' said Ellie helplessly. The despair she had felt when she had learnt that Jack was a father seemed so trivial compared with what he had gone through, and she ached with pity for him and the girl he had loved.

'That was the first I knew about Alice,' he said, as if the words were being torn from him. 'I couldn't take it in at first. All I knew was that Pippa was dead and that I hadn't been able to tell her how much I loved her.'

'Clare is Pippa's sister.' Seeing that Jack was struggling, Lizzy continued for him. 'Before Pippa died, she made Clare promise to bring Alice out to Australia so that she could grow up with Jack at Bushman's Creek.'

Ellie listened, but her attention was focused on Jack. His face was so bleak that she ached to comfort him, but there was nothing she could do and nothing she could say that would help.

'Clare kept her promise,' Lizzy was saying, 'but of

course by the time she got here Jack had gone. She and Gray looked after Alice together until he came home.'

'And now I *am* home,' said Jack. 'Gray and Clare have got their own life to lead, and I've got a daughter to look after.' He looked seriously at Ellie. 'I don't know what I'd have done when Clare left if it hadn't been for Lizzy.'

'You'd have learnt to change nappies even quicker than you have done!' Lizzy replied. 'And talking of changing nappies…'

She cocked an eye at the baby alarm, from where Alice's chattering had changed to a distinctly imperious shout, and Jack pushed back his chair with a rueful smile.

'I seem to be getting plenty of practice anyway,' he said. He glanced at Ellie. 'Do you want to come and meet my daughter?'

Ellie heard herself say that she would like that, and somehow managed to get to her feet. To her own surprise, her legs were quite steady as she followed Jack along the corridor.

Jack pushed open the door, and at the sight of him a baby with wisps of blond hair and a pair of cheeky brown eyes exactly like her father's broke into a beaming smile. She had hauled herself to her feet and was clutching the bars of the cot, her chubby little legs bouncing unsteadily up and down as she struggled valiantly to keep herself upright.

'Dada!' she shouted.

Jack swung her out of the cot, his big hands holding her securely up in the air, and the way he smiled lovingly up at his daughter before bringing her down to his face for a kiss made something ache deep inside Ellie. There was absolutely no doubt who held first place in Jack's heart now.

'This is Alice,' he said proudly, then sniffed cautiously

at her nappy. 'But I think I'd better change her before I introduce you properly!'

Ellie perched on an old toy box and watched as he laid Alice down on a table that had clearly been set up for just this purpose and unbuttoned her Babygro. It was obvious that the whole business of looking after a baby was new to him, but the tenderness and care with which he changed Alice's nappy were all the more moving for being so ham-fisted.

Watching Jack's harassed attempts to remove the dirty nappy, set a clean one in place and prevent Alice from rolling away to play with her toes, it seemed to Ellie that he had never been closer, nor, perversely, so out of reach. It was hard to imagine the old Jack changing a nappy, but now that the faint air of glamour which had clung to him in the past had been dulled by the preoccupations of fatherhood, he was no more likely to notice her than he had been before, when he had been the life and soul of the party.

Less, Ellie amended to herself. Jack's womanising days might be done, but he clearly had no thought for anything other than Alice and his bittersweet memories of Pippa. The faint hope that it would be her turn one day had gone. She would just have to accept that all she could ever be to Jack now was a friend.

And friends helped when they were needed.

Getting to her feet, Ellie wordlessly removed the dirty nappy from Jack's hapless grasp, disposed of it, and deftly fastened the clean one into place when he stood gratefully back.

'How do you make it look so easy?' he demanded as he wrestled with the poppers on the Babygro.

Ellie laughed. 'I've had lots of practice. Unlike Lizzy, I've always been a hands-on aunt, and I looked after several babies when I was a nanny in the States. There was a time when I could change nappies in my sleep.'

'I feel as if I'm doing that now,' Jack admitted ruefully. 'Only not as efficiently as you!'

He let Alice grab hold of his fingers and pulled her into a sitting position. 'I had no idea how exhausting it is to look after a baby,' he went on, looking over Alice's small blond head at Ellie. 'I think I had a vague idea you had to give them a bottle occasionally but otherwise they spent most of their time sleeping.

'I know better now, don't I?' he said to Alice, who burbled happily back at him. Finding her father conveniently at hand, she let go of his fingers and clutched at his shirt instead, using him as support to pull herself to her feet with a triumphant yell.

'I don't think I've ever been as tired as I've been this last month.' Jack's hands were ready to catch Alice the moment she lost her balance. 'I've had a crash course in fathering—and it's not even as if I've been able to spend all day with her. Lizzy's been the one who's really been looking after her.'

'Well, it looks as if you're doing a good job,' said Ellie. 'I never thought I'd see you change a nappy!'

'I know.' Jack grimaced. 'If you'd asked me two months ago if I wanted kids, I'd have said, No way! But the moment Clare put Alice in my arms it felt absolutely right.' He smoothed Alice's soft blond hair in a gesture of such tenderness that Ellie felt tears sting her eyes. 'Right, but scary. I've never been responsible for anyone before. She's so small and dependent. I'm terrified I won't be able to look after properly.'

'Of course you will,' said Ellie stoutly. 'Look at her! She's absolutely gorgeous!'

As if understanding, Alice looked over her shoulder at

Ellie and gave her a wide smile that showed off her four little teeth. 'Do you want to hold her?' offered Jack, scooping her up, and Ellie held out her arms.

'I'd love to,' she admitted.

Alice was a warm, solid weight, and Ellie cuddled her, loving her sweet baby smell. 'I love babies,' she confessed, and laughed as Alice explored her face with inquisitive little fingers. 'How old is she?'

'Ten months.' Jack's expression was suddenly sad. 'I've missed a lot of her life so far.'

'You're making up for it now, Jack,' said Ellie gently. 'She's happy and healthy and secure. You can't do more for her than that.'

'If she is, it's mostly due to Clare.' Jack wasn't ready to be reassured. 'She spent all her time with Alice, and I worry that I can't do the same. But with Gray away, I can't run the station and look after a baby. Lizzy's been fantastic, but I can't ask her to stay much longer. I know she's got plans to launch out into a business of her own, and she must be starting to think about going back to Perth soon.'

'I'm sure she'll stay until Clare gets back. It doesn't sound as if that'll be too long.'

'I know, but it's not fair to rely on Clare. She's done so much for Alice already, and she and Gray deserve some time on their own.' Jack picked up one of the toys Alice had thrown out of her cot and turned it absently between his fingers. 'I've been thinking about it a lot, and I've decided that Alice and I need to make a fresh start in a place of our own.'

Ellie rested her cheek against Alice's downy head. She could see that the idea made sense. 'Are you thinking of buying another property?'

'The old Murray place is up for sale,' he told her. 'Len

Murray died a couple of months ago, and his daughter isn't interested in the station. A lot of land to the north and east is being sold separately, but Waverley would still be a fair-sized property. It might be just what I'm looking for.'

'But, Jack, Len Murray was a virtual recluse,' Ellie protested, lifting her head in concern. 'I remember the last time Dad went over there, he said Len hadn't done any work on the station for fifteen years and everything was in a terrible state—and that was nearly five years ago. Things won't have improved since then.'

'It's worth a look,' said Jack stubbornly. 'Waverley Creek wouldn't be more than—what?—half an hour in a plane from here. I don't want to take Alice too far from Clare, and I can't think of anywhere else as convenient that's likely to come up for sale. I'm going to look at it tomorrow.'

He glanced at Ellie, who had settled Alice instinctively on her hip and was regarding him with a faint frown. 'Why don't you come with me?'

'Me?' she echoed in astonishment.

'You know more about running a station than most people,' Jack pointed out. 'You were always out mending fences and catching bulls when Lizzy was painting her nails and dreaming of the bright lights.'

'Yes, well, it turns out that Lizzy's experience is more useful than mine when it comes to getting a job,' sighed Ellie.

'Not to me,' said Jack. 'Much as I love Lizzy, I don't think she'd be much use when it comes to buying a cattle station. You'd know what you were looking at, and I could really do with a sensible opinion.'

He looked at her with a coaxing smile that crumbled

all her defences at a stroke. 'Come with me,' he pleaded. 'You could stop me doing something stupid!'

It wasn't fair of him to smile at her like that, thought Ellie, hugging Alice to her as if to ward off the force of his charm. If she were sensible, she would tell him she was busy. She would accept that Jack was never going to love her and she would go away and make herself forget him. She absolutely *wouldn't* torture herself by spending time with him and letting herself be sucked back into the old, terrible spiral of secret longing.

But could she really resist the prospect of a day by his side? Ellie asked herself honestly. So what if it was only because she could drive a truck and lasso a calf and talk knowledgeably about branding and breeding programmes? For the first time in all those long, hopeless years of dreaming she had a chance to be alone with Jack and know that he wanted her to be there.

So how sensible was she?

'Go on,' said Jack. 'You'll enjoy it.'

And Ellie succumbed to temptation, as she had known all along that she would.

'All right,' she said. 'I'd love to come.'

CHAPTER TWO

'WELL, what do you think?'

Ellie hesitated. There were a couple of chairs on the Waverley verandah, but, like everything else in the homestead, they were so old and rickety that she and Jack had elected to sit at the top of the verandah steps instead.

She thought of the homestead they had just finished inspecting, each room more depressingly grimy than the last, of the overgrown yards, broken fences and dilapidated sheds. 'It would be…a challenge,' she said at last.

Jack couldn't help grinning at the careful tact of her reply. 'You think I'm mad to even consider it, don't you, Ellie?'

'No,' she said surprisingly. 'This must have been a really nice property once, and it could be again—but it would take an awful lot of work.'

'I don't mind that. You don't have time to think when you're working.'

Ellie nodded, her eyes on the broken windmill. 'Sometimes it's easier that way,' she agreed.

The understanding in her voice made Jack glance at her curiously. It had been good to have her with him today. He had asked her to come on a whim, and had been surprised at how pleased he had been when she agreed.

Of course, he had always been fond of Ellie. He and Gray had grown up with Lizzy and Kevin, but Ellie had been much younger, a quiet little girl overshadowed by her boisterous brother and sister, only allowed to tag along on sufferance. Lizzy and Kevin had complained loudly about having to look after her, but he and Gray had never had a little sister, and, although they would have died rather than admit it at the time, they had found Ellie's open adoration rather appealing.

Now he found his gaze resting on her profile as she looked out at the ruined yards, lost in her own thoughts, and he wondered why she had ever needed to lose herself in work. For the first time it occurred to Jack how little he actually knew her. Ellie had always been a listener, not a talker. Even as a little girl, she could be relied upon to applaud his successes, admire his plans and sympathise with his woes, but she had never told him any of her own.

But then, thought Jack, he had never asked.

Suddenly he became aware that Ellie had turned her head and was looking at him, a question in her clear green eyes. 'Sorry,' he said, recollecting himself hurriedly. 'What did you say?'

'I just asked what *you* thought about Waverley.'

'I think I'd like to see a bit more before I make up my mind,' said Jack on impulse. He got to his feet, brushing the dust off his jeans. 'Shall we explore? I saw some saddles in one of the sheds, and those horses looked as if they could do with a ride.'

He set off with his long, easy stride towards the paddock, where a group of horses grazed in the sparse shade, their tails twitching against the flies. Ellie followed meekly, as she had done so often in the past.

'Do you think we should?' she asked dubiously when she caught up with Jack at the ramshackle fence.

'Why not?' he asked, and produced a piercing whistle that made the horses lift their heads and stare at them suspiciously.

'Well, it's not your property,' Ellie pointed out with a dry look. 'We ought to ask someone before we just waltz off with their horses.'

'There's no one to ask,' said Jack reasonably. 'And anyway, we're not taking the horses, we're just borrowing them for a while.'

He whistled again, and this time the horses succumbed to curiosity and came cantering over to inspect them. They shoved their heads over the fence, and Jack had to raise his voice over the sound of their whickered greetings.

'Who's going to mind? If I were the seller, I'd be more than happy to let anyone thinking seriously about taking this place off my hands do whatever they wanted, and if I were the horses, I'd be glad of the exercise!'

Seeing that Ellie was still looking unconvinced, he patted the neck of a big bay with a white blaze down its nose. 'What do you say, old fella? Do you want to show us Waverley Creek?'

The horse tossed its head up and down and snorted. 'There you are!' said Jack virtuously. 'He's dying to get out.'

It was typical of Jack that he could even get horses to do exactly what he wanted, thought Ellie, resigned, but she couldn't help laughing, and went off with him quite willingly to find the tack.

The horses didn't prove quite as eager to be ridden as Jack had so confidently predicted, but, like him, Ellie had been riding since she could walk, and she was more than capable of bringing her mount under control. After trying a few initial tricks, the horses settled down, and they headed quietly enough along the homestead creek, with only the occasional half-hearted buck or skittish sidestep to spoil the peace.

They picked their way through the trees that clustered along the banks of the creek. During the wet season it would be full, with an angry torrent, but it was long months since they had had any rain and the last of the water had collected in deep green pools. It was very still. Beyond the fractured shade, the heat shimmered over the red earth, wavering in the glare of the sun.

Ellie was very conscious of Jack riding beside her. He sat easily on the big bay, holding it in check with one hand while the other rested casually on his thigh. Oblivious to the birds that protested at their approach, wheeling and squawking in indignant crowds before settling back into the branches above their heads in huffy silence, he was assessing the land with narrowed brown eyes. Jack might have been the life and soul of every party in the district, but that didn't mean he didn't know just as much about what it took to run a successful cattle station as the other, less social graziers.

Content to let Jack worry about yields and crops and acreages, Ellie breathed in the scent of dust and hot, dry leaves, and gave herself up to the pleasure of being with him. Last night, lying alone in the bed she had slept in since she was a child, she had given herself a severe talking-to. It was time to stop dreaming. Jack was grieving for Pippa, and had more than enough to worry about adjusting to fatherhood. He wasn't ready to think about love again, and he might never be.

She couldn't stop loving him, but she could stop dreaming she would ever be more to him than a friend, and right now, riding beneath the trees in the hot hush of afternoon, with Jack close beside her, friendship was enough for Ellie. She felt alert and alive in a way she hadn't for three long years. She could smell the drifting fragrance of eucalyptus in the air, mingled with the scent of red dust and horse and the leather on her hands. She could hear the horses' hooves, the jingle of the bit, the galahs squabbling in the treetops.

Most of all, she could see Jack, outlined in heart-wrenching clarity against the trees on the far side of the creek. It was as if only now she could let herself believe that he was really there, and her senses tingled with awareness of every tiny detail about him: his fingers around the reins, the glint of hairs at his wrist, the slanting shadow cast by the brim of his hat.

Turning his head, Jack saw her smile and he lifted his brows. 'You look happy,' he commented.

A faint flush stole up Ellie's cheeks. 'I'm just glad to be home again,' she said, and, afraid that the expression in her eyes would betray her, she looked around her at the quiet creek.

'I missed all this so much when I was away. I was homesick for three years,' she confessed with a shame-faced smile. 'Sometimes I'd close my eyes and wish that I was home, somewhere just like this, and every time when I opened them again and found that I wasn't, I wanted to cry.'

Ellie stopped, aware that she had said more than she had meant to, but Jack didn't appear to have guessed that he had always been there in her dream. When she glanced at him, she found that he was watching her, a faint frown between his brows.

'Why didn't you come home if you missed it that badly?' he asked her, vaguely disturbed by how much he hated the idea of Ellie being miserable and alone.

'I thought about it lots of times, but I knew that if I did I'd just end up having to get a job in the city, like Lizzy, and that wouldn't have been any better. I only ever wanted to be in the outback.'

With you, she added mentally, knowing that she could never tell Jack that.

'But couldn't you have gone home? It's not as if you wouldn't be a useful person to have around,' said Jack, puzzled. 'There must have been lots for you to do on the station.'

'I could have done, but Mum and Dad retired last year. They're still living on the station, but there isn't a lot of room in their new house, and although I can always stay in the homestead with Kevin and Sue, I don't think it's fair on them to have me hanging around permanently. It's fine to come back for a visit, but it's their home now, not mine.'

Concerned, Jack turned in his saddle to study her. 'So what are you going to do?'

'I'm not quite sure.' Ellie shrugged slightly and tried to laugh. 'Ideally, I'd find a job here, but Mathison isn't exactly full of career opportunities. It would be different if I could do something useful, like fly a helicopter, but I can't.' She sighed. 'I could be a station hand or a housekeeper, I suppose, but those kind of jobs are only ever seasonal, and I'd never be able to call anywhere home.'

Jack was frowning. 'It's not fair on you. I know Lizzy couldn't wait to head for the city, but it's different for you. Couldn't you and Kevin have run the station together?'

'Not once Kevin married Sue. Sue's great, and she's always really welcoming, but it's their property and they need to get on and run it their way.'

'I still don't think it's fair,' said Jack stubbornly, and she smiled faintly.

'It's just the way things are, Jack. I don't think it ever occurred to Dad that Lizzy and I wouldn't marry nice local boys and end up on their properties!'

Jack ran a mental eye over all the eligible men in the district. He could think of a few who could do with a capable wife like Ellie, although none who would be good enough for her. 'Perhaps it'll still happen,' he said, even though the thought gave him a strangely hollow feeling.

Ellie kept her eyes fixed between the horse's ears and smiled a brief, mechanical smile. 'Perhaps,' she said.

They rode in silence for a while, until they came to a place where the water had collected in a deep pool between the rocks and the trees leant over to admire their reflections in its still surface.

'Let's stop here,' said Jack.

He tied the horses up in the shade while Ellie sat on a rock worn smooth and red with time. Taking off her hat, she ran her fingers through her wavy brown hair and leant back on her hands with a sigh of contentment. Sheltered from the outback glare, the waterhole seemed to her a peaceful, almost magical place, but the tranquil atmosphere appeared lost on Jack.

He prowled restlessly around the water's edge, lobbing in an occasional stone to gauge its depth. 'I could teach Alice to swim here,' he said as he hunkered down to test the temperature of the water with his hand. 'It reminds me of the waterhole at home. We used to swim there all the time when we were kids.'

'I remember,' said Ellie. 'I used to love our visits to Bushman's Creek.'

'We had some good times, didn't we?' Jack straightened, his nostalgic smile fading. 'I want Alice to grow up with those kind of memories,' he said seriously.

'She will, Jack.'

'What if she's lonely?' The worried look was back in Jack's eyes as he came to sit next to Ellie on her rock.

'You had Lizzy and Kevin, and I had Gray, but Alice won't have anyone to play with in the same way.'

Leaning forward, he rested his arms on his thighs, holding his hat loosely between his knees as he gazed abstractedly across the water. 'Waverley Creek's got a lot of problems, but it feels like the right station for me,' he said. 'I'm just not sure if it's the right place for Alice.'

Ellie was very conscious of his nearness, and of the fact that Jack was quite unaware of hers. It meant nothing to him that her thigh was barely inches away from his, or that by leaning very slightly together their shoulders would touch. He was preoccupied with more important matters, like his daughter's future.

'The right place for Alice is wherever you are, Jack,' she told him, wishing the same could be true for her.

'Even if it means growing up on her own?'

Ellie's eyes rested on the dust between the rocks, where she was tracing a pattern with the heel of her boot. 'You might meet someone else,' she made herself suggest. 'You could have more children.'

'I don't want to meet anyone else.' Jack's voice was flat and final. 'What Pippa and I had was special. How could I expect to find a love like that again?'

'Maybe you'll find a different kind of love,' said Ellie, without lifting her gaze from the dust at her feet, and she sensed rather than saw Jack's involuntary recoil at the very idea.

'Easy for you to say,' he said harshly. 'You've never been in love.'

'Yes, I have.'

Jack was taken aback at the edge to the quiet voice, and he turned his head to look at Ellie curiously. She sounded almost bitter, he thought. Surely she was too young to sound like that?

He did a quick calculation in his head and realised with
something of a shock that she must be at least twenty-
five. Plenty old enough to learn about disappointment and
regret and heartache. It just seemed odd to think of little
Ellie in love, Jack decided. She had always been such a
tomboy.

She still was. He thought of how she had looked when
he had picked her up this morning. She had been waiting
for him at the airstrip, perched on the bonnet of an old
ute, looking trim and practical in jeans and an old blue
shirt. No bag, no sunglasses, no lipstick, no fuss, Jack
had noted with approval. Just a hat in her hand, and she
was ready to go. Good old Ellie; she was always the
same.

He glanced at her affectionately, but she was looking
away, and he found himself studying her averted face
with amusement that faded into a dawning sense of puzzlement.

Had Ellie always had such smooth honey-coloured
skin? And where had that delicate bone structure come
from? Jack felt oddly unsettled. It was like running up to
someone you knew, only to discover at the last moment
that they were a stranger after all. This was the same Ellie
who had jumped off the ute to greet him, but suddenly
she didn't look like a tomboy at all.

Jack's eyes drifted down to her mouth and he frowned.
No, not at all.

'I didn't know,' he said slowly, wondering when she
had changed, and why he had never noticed before.

'Why should you?' Ellie spoke lightly, but she kept
her face averted.

What kind of man would Ellie fall in love with?
thought Jack. What kind of man had stirred the passion
banked beneath her quiet surface? Whoever it was, he

had changed her from a tomboy into someone disturbingly unfamiliar. Was it the same man who had caused the bitterness in her voice?

'Was it someone you met in the States?' he couldn't help asking.

At first he thought that Ellie wasn't going to answer, but then she shook her head. 'No,' she said in a low voice. 'I went to the States to forget him.'

'And did you?'

Ellie turned slowly until she was looking straight at him, and Jack found himself noticing as if for the first time that her eyes were a beautiful colour, somewhere between grey and green, and very clear.

'No,' she said at last. 'I tried to, but I couldn't.'

'He must be someone special.' There was an odd note in Jack's voice. He was intrigued by the idea of Ellie being in love, but it left him feeling peculiarly ruffled at the same time.

Ellie dropped her eyes, a faint smile just touching the corners of her mouth. 'He is.'

'So, is that why you've come home?' demanded Jack, unable to account for the harshness in his tone. 'To try and work things out with him?'

Her smile faded. 'There's nothing *to* work out. He's not in love with me, and I know that he never will be. It's just a dream, and I've accepted that, but it doesn't stop me loving him. I didn't come home expecting anything to happen,' she told him, almost as if she needed to reassure him. 'I just thought it would be easier being in the same place, that's all.'

'Poor Ellie.' Jack reached over and squeezed her hand. '*You* need to find someone different, too.'

'I know.' To her horror, Ellie felt tears sting her eyes, and she blinked fiercely as she tugged her hand away.

Jack's sympathy was harder to bear than anything else. His clasp was warm and comforting, but it wasn't comfort she wanted from him. 'But you were right; it isn't that easy.'

'No,' he agreed soberly. 'At least you understand how I feel about Pippa. I can't imagine loving anyone else the way I loved her. I know it sounds corny, but it's as if I found the other half of me, and now I've lost it again.'

When Ellie stole a glance at him, he was staring down at the ground beneath his feet, his expression very bleak. 'No one else can take Pippa's place,' he went on after a moment. 'Anyone I met now would have to accept only ever being second best, and I could never ask anyone to do that.'

Ellie's heart twisted at his words, but she knew exactly how he felt. She had tried so hard to fall in love with other men, but deep down she had always known that it would be hopeless. No matter how nice or attractive or charming they were, they would never match up to Jack. Only he would do.

'Yes, I do understand,' she said quietly.

Jack looked up at that, his eyes dark and brown and sad, and his smile rather twisted. 'It looks like we're in the same boat,' he said.

'At least you've got memories.' I've only ever had dreams, Ellie added bitterly to herself. She hadn't lost what Jack had, but she had never known the joy of being loved by him either. 'And you've got Alice.'

'Yes, I've got Alice.' Jack sighed and got restlessly to his feet once more. 'And it's because of Alice that I need to forget about how I feel and think seriously about meeting someone else and getting married. If I don't, she's going to grow up with a succession of housekeepers. She needs a mother, not someone who'll stay for a few weeks or a few months and then get bored or tired of the conditions and go to work somewhere easier.'

'It doesn't have to be like that, does it?'

'No,' he agreed, 'but it probably would be. You know how hard it is to get good, reliable people to stay in the outback. Anyone with any sense would take one look at the homestead back there and head straight back to the town.'

Hunching his shoulders, Jack frowned across the creek. 'I don't think buying Waverley Creek is going to work, Ellie. It's a fine station—or it could be—but perhaps it would be better for Alice if we stayed at Bushman's Creek after all.'

'But you don't want to do that,' Ellie objected, and he sighed as he ran his hand through his hair in a gesture of weariness.

'No, I don't. Quite apart from anything else, it wouldn't be fair on Gray and Clare. But my only alternative is to find myself a wife…and where am I going to find someone who'd be prepared to take on me and Alice and Pippa's ghost?'

He was standing with his back to Ellie, arguing with himself more than with her, and she looked at him with a peculiar mixture of pain and pleasure. The back of his head was utterly familiar to her, and she let her eyes travel longingly from his broad shoulders to the lean hips and down the long legs.

It was wonderful just to be near him. All that time in the States, when she had longed to see him again, and now here he was, and she had to face what she had known all along, that he would never love her the way she loved him. She had dreaded the time that Jack would fall in love, and it hurt just as she had feared that it would…but could she bear to go away again and not see him for another three years?

No, thought Ellie, I can't. Anything would be better than that.

She drew a deep breath. 'What about here?' she asked, before she had a chance to lose her nerve.

'Here?' Jack glanced over his shoulder at Ellie, sitting defensively straight on her rock. She was braced against his scorn, but his expression was half-abstracted, half-puzzled, and he was clearly wondering if he had heard her properly.

'You could marry me,' she heard her voice saying.

Jack swung round at that, to stare blankly at her. 'Marry *you*?' he echoed.

He sounded so incredulous that Ellie flinched. For a moment she was tempted to pretend that she was only joking, but a still, clear voice inside her told her that this would be her only chance. She had got this far, so she might as well see it through, and if Jack laughed or recoiled in disgust, well, at least she would have tried.

'You want someone to live permanently at Waverley Creek and help you look after Alice,' she said, amazed at her own calm control. 'I want to stay permanently in the outback. The conditions here won't bother me, and I'm not likely to get bored like other girls you might get from an agency.'

Jack eyed her uncertainly. His smile had faltered as he realised with a shock that she was quite serious. 'Ellie,' he said rather helplessly, 'I can't marry you.'

'Why not?'

'Because…' Thrown by the directness of the question, Jack raked his fingers through his hair. Surely it was obvious? 'Because…'

'Because you don't love me? I know that.'

'I think I was trying to say because you don't love *me*.'

'Then we're in the same boat,' said Ellie, 'just like you said.'

'But, Ellie, why would you want to marry a man you don't love?' asked Jack, still struggling to come to terms with her extraordinary suggestion.

It was Ellie's turn to get to her feet. Unable to sit still any longer, she went to stand by the edge of the waterhole, where she could look into his face without crowding him. 'I want to stay in the outback,' she told him simply.

Jack's brown eyes narrowed. 'To be near this man you're so in love with?'

'Partly,' she said carefully. 'Partly because I want to belong somewhere. I don't want to have to go to work in the city and just come back for occasional visits. I want a home of my own here, a place I could have a stake in. If I married you, I could help you build up Waverley into a great station again.'

Jack wasn't looking convinced, and she hurried on before he had a chance to turn her down flat.

'Think about it, Jack. A marriage of convenience might not be what either of us wanted, but it could work. I know how you feel about Pippa. You wouldn't have to pretend with me, and I…I wouldn't expect anything from you that you couldn't give.' Ellie tried a smile. 'You'd get stability for Alice, and a free housekeeper on a permanent basis!'

'And what would you get?' asked Jack slowly.

'Security,' she said. 'I haven't got any money, Jack. There's no way I could afford to buy and run a station of my own, and I haven't got any other skills to make a place for myself. The only way I could stay in the outback is to get a job where I'd be completely dependent on someone else…or to marry.'

It seemed so bizarre to be standing at the creek edge, calmly discussing marriage with little Ellie Walker, that Jack shook his head slightly to shake off the feeling of unreality. She had to be desperately unhappy to even think of such an idea, he realised in concern.

'Ellie,' he said, taking her hand, 'you're young. Too young to tie yourself to a man you don't love. You'll meet someone else eventually.'

'I won't, Jack,' she said, and her gaze was very steady. 'There's only ever going to be one man for me.'

'You seem very sure that he doesn't love you,' said Jack, picking his words with care. He let go of her hand. 'What if he changes his mind?'

'He's not going to do that.' Ellie smiled a little sadly. 'I've wasted enough of my life hoping that one day he'd notice me and fall in love with me, but I think it's time I faced reality.'

Her eyes slid away from his, and she turned her head slightly so that Jack shouldn't read the truth in her face.

'I've accepted that it's not going to happen the way I wanted,' she said, 'but I know, too, that I'll never be happy away from him. At least if I married you I'd be able to be near him.' Her voice cracked and she stopped abruptly, afraid that she had already revealed too much.

Jack's eyes rested curiously on her averted face. 'Who is it, Ellie?' he asked, wanting to know but unsurprised when she only shook her head.

'I can't tell you.'

'You don't think that if we got married I'd have a right to know?'

'No.' She still wouldn't look at him. 'It wouldn't make any difference.'

'But it's someone you'd see if you lived with me here?' he persisted.

'Sometimes, yes,' she said cagily.

'It would be easier to make a fresh start,' said Jack gently. 'Being married to me, seeing him but not being able to be with him...that would be very hard.'

'Not as hard as not seeing him at all,' said Ellie. 'I'd have a home, somewhere to belong, and I'd know that I wouldn't have to go away again. I'd have Alice and a chance to share in Waverley. I think it would be enough.'

Jack rubbed a hand over his face and tried to think clearly. 'I don't know, Ellie. It's a crazy idea.'

He stared into the water and thought irrelevantly that it was almost exactly the colour of Ellie's eyes, very green in the sunlight but shading into grey in the shadows, just as her eyes had darkened with unhappiness. Marrying Ellie...it *was* a crazy idea. He couldn't believe that he was even thinking about it.

But he was.

There was no denying that marriage would solve a lot of his problems, and although it would never have occurred to him to think about Ellie before, in many ways she would be ideal. She was practical and sensible, someone you could rely on not to make a fuss or complain or panic when things when wrong.

She would be good for Alice, too. Jack remembered how calmly she had changed Alice's nappy, how she had cuddled her, the easy way she had settled her on her hip. Ellie knew how to deal with babies, and she knew how to deal with cattle.

She wasn't anything like Pippa, of course, but perhaps that would make it easier. Ellie understood exactly how he felt about Pippa, so he wouldn't have to pretend to be in love with her, the way he might have to with someone else. Jack didn't think he could bear to do that.

With Ellie, he would never have to pretend. He could say what he felt, be the way he wanted, and know that she would always accept him, and make no demands on him in return. Yes, she would be an easy person to live with. She wasn't Pippa, but she was a friend. There might be worse marriages.

He stood gazing into the water for so long that Ellie began to lose her nerve. She must have been mad to even suggest it, she thought in panic, and her cheeks burned as the full enormity of what she had done sank in.

Things would never be the same between her and Jack again. He was bound to guess that she was grasping at any chance to be with him. He would feel awkward and embarrassed and would avoid her whenever he could, and she might as well have stayed in the States for all she would see of him.

Why hadn't she thought before she opened her mouth? Ellie asked herself miserably. There was no way Jack would ever marry her. She should have left things the way they were and accepted that she would only ever be a friend. Now he was standing there trying to think of a kind way to tell her that she was the last person he would ever consider marrying.

'Look, forget I mentioned it,' she blurted out at last, unable to bear the silence any longer. 'It was just a silly idea.'

'No, it's not silly,' said Jack to her surprise, and he turned back to face her. 'It's not silly at all.'

Ellie swallowed. 'But?' she asked, hearing the hesitation in his voice.

'But we both need time to think about what getting

married would mean. Marriage is a big step, and we don't want to rush into anything we might both regret.'

'So what are you suggesting?' Ellie's voice was calm, but inside she was trembling wildly at the realisation that he hadn't turned her down flat after all.

'That we wait until after the Wet,' said Jack. 'I'm going to put in an offer to buy Waverley Creek, but it's going to need a lot of work over the next two or three months just to make the homestead habitable. If you stay at home with Kevin and Sue, you could come over and help me.'

He hesitated. 'It seems stupid to say that we need to get to know each other better when we've always known each other, but it might give us a chance to get used to the idea of being married—and a chance to change our minds if we don't think it would work after all. We could spend the wet season working on the homestead together, and then if we both still think it's a good idea, we could get engaged then. Does that sound fair to you?'

'Yes,' said Ellie, hardly daring to believe that Jack was really considering marrying her. 'It sounds very fair.'

In a daze, she picked up her hat and followed Jack over to where the horses waited patiently, twitching their tails against the flies. She let him untie them and took the reins he handed her with the same sense of glorious disbelief.

'I don't think we should tell anyone what we talked about today,' said Jack as he settled his own hat on his head. 'Not even Lizzy.'

'Definitely not Lizzy,' Ellie agreed quickly. Lizzy would be appalled if she knew that her sister was prepared to marry a man who didn't love her, and she would do everything in her power to dissuade her. 'What will

you tell her?' she asked, worried that Lizzy would somehow guess what they had discussed anyway.

'Just that we had a good time.' Jack watched her swing
herself easily onto the horse and smiled. 'It's true, too. I
did.'

He *had* had a good time, he realised with a sense of
surprise. Ellie was a very restful person to be with. Somehow she made things seem not only possible, but simple.

The future was suddenly looking much brighter than
he would have believed possible when he had left
Bushman's Creek that morning, weighed down by worries about Alice and what to do for the best. Now he had
not only made a decision about buying Waverley Creek,
but Ellie had come up with an amazing solution to the
problem of how to care for his daughter.

Jack was conscious of a rush of gratitude. The marriage idea might not work out—he couldn't help thinking
that Ellie would change her mind when she thought about
it—but at least he was thinking positively about the future now, and for the first time since he had learnt of
Pippa's death it seemed less bleak and less lonely. That
was due to Ellie.

'I'm glad you came with me today, Ellie,' he said seriously.

Ellie looked down into his warm brown eyes, and her
heart melted at the thought that if she married him she
would be able to look into them every day.

'So am I,' she said.

CHAPTER THREE

'THERE!' Ellie stood back to admire her handiwork. 'That's the window finished in here.'

She smiled down at Alice, who was having a lovely time banging an old brush around inside an empty paint tin, and gestured at the window with her own paintbrush. 'What do you think, Alice?'

Alice looked up at the sound of her own name, and her face split into an adorably mischievous grin that showed off her two bottom teeth. She was the most sociable baby Ellie had ever met, and loved to talk, chattering away in her own incomprehensible language whenever anyone spoke to her. She jabbered approvingly in reply to Ellie now, and thumped her brush against the wooden floorboards as if for added emphasis.

'That means that she thinks it looks great,' said Jack's voice from behind her, and Ellie swung round.

He was leaning casually against the doorframe in a paint-splattered shirt, wiping his hands with a rag and watching her and his small daughter with amusement. Ellie's heart turned over. The two of them had been working together on the homestead at Waverley Creek for the last couple of months, but her insides still jerked themselves into a ridiculous knot whenever she caught sight of him unexpectedly.

Alice shouted with delight as she spotted her father, and she threw the paintbrush and can aside to crawl eagerly across the floorboards and clutch at the bottom of his jeans. Jack let her clamber unsteadily to her feet, us-

41

ing his legs as a support, before he swung her up into his arms and tossed her high in the air, shrieking with excitement.

Ellie couldn't help laughing. She loved seeing Jack and Alice together. They so obviously adored each other that it was impossible to resent the fact that there was no room in Jack's heart for anyone other than his baby daughter.

'What's she saying now?' she teased him.

Jack caught Alice in his big hands and bent his head towards hers, nodding solemnly as he pretended to understand her excited babble. 'She wants to know why you're still working,' he announced.

'I just wanted to finish the window,' Ellie explained. She put her brush into a jar of turpentine and hunted around for a rag to clean the worst of the paint from her hands. 'How are you getting on in the kitchen?'

'I've finished. Come and see.'

'Oh, Jack, it looks wonderful!' Ellie exclaimed a few moments later as she stood in the middle of the kitchen. It was hard to believe that it was the same room they had inspected with such dismay two months ago. Then, it had been dingy and depressing, encrusted with dust and dirt. Now, with everything scrubbed clean and freshly painted, it had been transformed into a bright, welcoming room.

'It looks a lot better, doesn't it?'

Pleased with her reaction, Jack stood Alice on the worktop and held her hands so that she could balance on her wobbly little legs.

'Gah, gah, boo, *ma*!' she cried, thrilled.

'You're quite right as usual, Alice,' said Jack seriously. 'It *is* time for a beer!'

Ellie laughed, but stole a glance at her watch. 'I could start the window in Alice's bedroom,' she began.

'Oh, no, you couldn't,' he said firmly. 'You've been

working all day, and you've done enough. Here,' he went on, sweeping Alice up and depositing her in Ellie's arms. 'You take Alice and stop arguing. I'll find the beers.'

Ellie was pleasantly weary, and not that sorry to be bullied into carrying Alice out onto the verandah and sitting down for a while. The furniture that had been left in the homestead when Jack bought it had been so old and dirty that Jack had thrown the whole lot away, but he had brought over a couple of canvas chairs and a folding table, where they sat and had lunch or a beer when they had finished work for the day, and Ellie was looking forward to taking the weight off her feet.

She set Alice on the wooden floor and gave her a toy from the bag that Jack had brought with him that morning. He liked to have Alice with him whenever he could, and since he had been spending as much time as possible at Waverley Creek Ellie had got to know his small daughter, and was well on her way to being as besotted by her as Jack himself.

For Ellie, the last two months had been a magical time. It had been wonderful to be home, to be doing something useful, and although cleaning the homestead had been hot, back-breaking work, she had enjoyed seeing the old house come back to life before her eyes.

And then, of course, there was Jack. Ellie didn't care how hard she worked as long as she could sit with him on the verandah here at the end of the day and talk.

They were friends, better friends than they had been before, but still just friends, and she had accepted long ago that Jack wasn't looking for any more than that. Kevin and Sue had begun to raise their eyebrows and comment on the amount of time she and Jack were spending together, but although they had camped overnight in the homestead once or twice, so that they could get more work done, he had treated her exactly as he would a sister.

Jack had never mentioned the idea of marriage again, and Ellie was reluctant to raise the subject in case he had changed his mind. She couldn't bear to think about what would happen if he had. It would mean no more days at Waverley Creek, no more Alice, with her naughty brown eyes and gorgeous smile, no more Jack.

Ellie closed her mind to the very thought. Refusing to consider the future, she was content to be with Jack while she could, storing up memories of sitting alone with him in the dark, of seeing him smile and knowing that there was no one else for miles and miles around.

'Here you are.'

She started as Jack appeared with beers in polystyrene beakers to keep them cold. He handed her one, then squatted down to offer Alice a drink in her special cup. She cast her toy aside and took the cup instantly, her little hands clutching the two handles as she guzzled noisily, her lids with their absurdly long lashes drooping contentedly.

Jack watched her for a moment with a faint smile, then straightened to lean against the verandah rail, facing Ellie. 'Here's to you, Ellie,' he said, raising his beer to her. 'Thank you.'

She glanced up at him in surprise. 'For what?'

'For everything,' he said seriously. 'Do you think I haven't noticed how hard you've worked over the last two months?'

He looked around at the scrubbed verandah and the freshly painted windows. 'This is going to be a nice house when it's finished. If it wasn't for you, I wouldn't be here at all. I certainly wouldn't be able to think about moving in yet.'

Ellie put down her beer and looked at him in consternation. 'You're not thinking about moving in already?'

'We've just got Alice's room to finish,' Jack pointed out. 'The others can wait until we've got more time. It may not be very grand, but at least the house is liveable now. I don't see why we shouldn't move in as soon as possible.'

We? thought Ellie. Did that mean Jack and Alice, or was she included too?

All at once the golden afternoon seemed to dim. Jack was getting impatient, and that meant things were going to change. For better, for worse... Whatever happened, this magical time when she hadn't needed to think about the future was about to end.

Restlessly, Ellie got to her feet. 'I didn't realise you were thinking of moving so soon,' she said.

'Gray and Clare have been back over a month now,' said Jack. 'They're both wonderful with Alice, and there's no denying things are easier with Clare there, but...' He hesitated. 'Well, the fact is that it's harder than I thought it would be. They're so in love, just like Pippa and I were. Sometimes it hurts to see them.'

He turned round to lean his arms on the verandah rail, and his brown gaze rested unseeingly on the distant horizon. 'It's not that they spend their time kissing and cuddling, far from it. It's just the way I see them look at each other, the way they seem to belong together.'

Ellie leant next to him on the rail. 'I can understand that it must be difficult for you,' she said quietly. 'Clare and Pippa were sisters, weren't they? Does she remind you of Pippa?'

'Sometimes,' said Jack. 'She doesn't look anything like Pippa, but every now and then she says something, or turns her head in a certain way, and then it's as if Pippa's standing right in front of me again.'

His mouth twisted painfully. 'You know, a lot of the time I can make myself believe that things are just the way they were before, that Pippa's back in England, just waiting for me to go and apologise for that stupid argument we had. But when I see Clare use the same kind of mannerisms, it brings it all home somehow. Clare wouldn't be here if it wasn't for Pippa, and Pippa is dead.'

'Oh, Jack,' said Ellie helplessly, and when Jack looked into her warm green eyes he felt ashamed for upsetting her.

'Don't look like that, Ellie,' he said, putting his hand over hers, as if she was the one who needed comforting rather than him. 'It's not that bad most of the time. It's not fair of me to complain. It sounds as if I resent Gray's marriage, and I don't at all. I'm really glad that he's found Clare, and that the two of them are so happy together. I just think it would be easier if Alice and I lived here, that's all.'

Alice and I, Ellie noted dully. No one else. 'I see,' she said.

Jack read disapproval into her comment. 'Obviously I won't bring Alice over until everything's ready for her,' he tried to reassure her, 'but I hope it won't be too long now—thanks to you and all the work you've been doing here.'

Ellie mustered a smile. 'I'm glad I could help.'

'You've certainly done that. I could never have done it without you,' said Jack sincerely. He looked out at the land with satisfaction. 'Only another week or so, and this will be home.' Glancing at Ellie with a sudden, boyish smile, he admitted, 'I can't wait!'

She kept her eyes on the dusty track that shimmered off into the distance. 'So you move to Waverley. What happens then, Jack?'

'A lot more work.' Jack sounded as if he relished the prospect.

'And with Alice?'

'That's up to you, Ellie.' He turned slightly to look at her as she leant on the rail beside him. 'It's hard to believe that it's only a couple of months since we first came to Waverley. Do you remember that day?'

The memory of it was engrained on her heart. 'Of course,' she said, not looking at him.

'I've been thinking a lot about that conversation we had down at the creek,' said Jack.

Ellie's mouth was very dry. 'And?'

'And I think that marrying you would be a very good thing—for me,' he said slowly. 'It would be good for Alice, too. I'm just not sure it would be so good for you.'

'Isn't that for me to decide?'

'I don't want you to do anything you might regret,' he told her, choosing his words with care, and he smiled slightly. 'You're a useful person to have around, Ellie. You would solve all my domestic problems, but all I can offer in return is a lot of hard work bringing up a baby and getting this station back onto its feet.'

'And the chance to stay where I belong and do what I love doing,' she pointed out. 'It seems a fair exchange to me.'

Jack shook his head. 'You deserve more than that.' He paused. 'You said that you wanted security, and I *can* give you that. As my wife you'd be entitled to a half-share in Waverley, and if you wanted to leave I'd have to buy you out. You wouldn't need to worry about money again.'

Ellie straightened in consternation. 'I didn't mean financial security, Jack,' she protested. 'I just want to be somewhere I could stay. There's no need for you to give me anything.'

'I don't think you realise quite what it's going to mean to me to have you here,' he said, regarding her with a quizzical air. 'It's all very well to talk about employing people to help, but the more I thought about living at Waverley, the more I realised that I couldn't do it without you. A financial stake in the station is the least you deserve! Quite apart from anything else, think of all the money you're going to save me in wages for housekeepers and cooks and nannies!'

Ellie didn't smile back. 'I wish you wouldn't do it, Jack,' she said, hugging her arms together as if to ward off his generosity. 'It makes me uncomfortable just to think about it.'

'Then don't think about it,' said Jack. 'You just need to know that it's there, and you might as well get used to the idea because it's one of my conditions. If you won't accept it, I won't marry you.'

There was a note of finality in his voice that gave Ellie pause, and she eyed him uncertainly. She hated the idea of benefiting financially from marriage when all she had ever wanted was to be with Jack, but he was so stubborn that she wouldn't put it past him to do exactly what he said and refuse to marry her unless she agreed.

Jack read her expression without difficulty. 'Don't be so proud,' he said with a touch of exasperation. 'It's not as if I'm buying you.'

'That's what it feels like,' she said a little bitterly.

'Ellie, be sensible,' he said more gently. 'If we were getting married under normal circumstances, you wouldn't think twice about sharing in all my worldly goods, would you?'

Ellie kept her face carefully expressionless. 'But they're not normal circumstances, are they, Jack?'

'No,' he agreed. 'I think we should treat our marriage as a proper partnership. We won't be a normal husband and wife, but we can be partners, and to do that we need to have equal shares in Waverley.'

'All right,' said Ellie after a moment. There was obviously no point in arguing further, and anyway, it wasn't as if she would ever want to sell her share. She would only ever own half of Waverley on paper.

'Thank you,' she added, uncomfortably aware that she had sounded more than a little ungracious for someone who had just been promised half a cattle station.

'I do have one other condition,' said Jack.

She eyed him warily. 'What's that?'

'That if you ever want out of the marriage, you'll tell me. You may not feel now that there's any hope for you with this man that you're in love with,' he went on quickly, as she opened her mouth to protest, 'but things might change. I don't want you to feel trapped, Ellie, or that you've lost your chance at happiness. You have to promise me that if you *do* ever feel like that, you'll say. I'll let you go without any hard feelings.'

Of course he would. Ellie turned her face away and fought down the hurt twisting in her guts. She knew that Jack was trying to be kind. He couldn't know that every time he made it clear that he didn't love her, her heart cracked a little more.

'It's only fair,' he urged her when she didn't say anything, and Ellie swallowed.

It wasn't as if she didn't know how Jack felt. If she didn't like the fact that he wasn't in love with her and wasn't even going to pretend that he was, she should back out now. There was no point in expecting something from him that he couldn't give.

'It's only fair if you'll tell me, too,' she said, marvelling at how cool and unconcerned she sounded. 'We'll be partners, just like you said, not a real husband and wife. If there ever comes a time when you fall in love again, I hope you'll let me know.'

Forcing herself to meet his eyes, Ellie went on, 'We should make it part of our agreement that if either of us wants to end our marriage, the other won't contest it.'

Jack considered the matter, although she was sure that she had seen a flicker of relief in his eyes. 'If that's what you want,' he said at last, and then he held out his hand. 'Shall we shake on it?'

After the tiniest of hesitations, Ellie put her hand into his and felt his fingers close around hers. The touch of his flesh sent a throb of response through her, warming her blood and tingling just beneath her skin.

The effect was so disturbing that she made to draw her hand away, but Jack kept a firm hold of it. 'Now that we've agreed on all that, perhaps we can agree on the most important thing,' he said, with a smile that made her heart thud with painful intensity against her ribs. 'Will you marry me, Ellie?'

How odd, thought Ellie. She had imagined this scene so many times, but she didn't feel at all as she had always expected. Irrelevantly, she found herself remembering her grandmother's favourite saying: Don't wish too hard for what you want, or you will surely get it.

All she had ever wanted was to marry Jack, and now here he was, asking her to do just that, and all she could feel was a faint, poignant sadness that life never turned out quite the way you expected it to. In her dreams, Jack wanted to marry her because he loved her the way she desperately loved him, but this was real life, and she couldn't help wishing that he wanted her as a wife and not as a friend, as a lover instead of a useful person to have around.

He was waiting for her to answer. Ellie looked into his warm brown eyes with their lurking smile and felt her sudden doubts dissolve in a familiar clench of longing. So what if it wasn't perfect, the way she had dreamt it would be? At least she would be with him. It would be enough.

She took a steadying breath. 'Yes,' she said, 'I will.'

Jack hadn't missed her hesitation, and his clasp tightened. 'Are you sure?' he asked, only half teasing.

'I'm sure.'

'Good,' said Jack, his smile fading slowly as he looked down into Ellie's face. Her brown hair was pushed anyhow behind her ears and there was a smudge of paint on her cheek, but the grey-green eyes were clear and true.

His gaze dropped to her mouth, and without warning he found himself wondering what it would be like to kiss her. She had just said that she would marry him. Wouldn't it be the most natural thing in the world to kiss her?

What was he thinking of? Jack caught himself up guiltily. It might be natural to kiss under normal circumstances, but the circumstances weren't normal. This was Ellie, the closest thing he had to a kid sister. Ellie, who was in love with another man and who had made it clear that their marriage would be a purely businesslike arrangement.

And that was what he wanted too, Jack reminded himself. Marrying Ellie would only work if they could stay friends, and the best way to do that was not to complicate matters by kissing her.

On the other hand, they *were* going to get married. He could hardly just shake her hand again, could he?

'Good,' he said again, and bent his head to kiss her cheek instead. It was a nice, safe compromise, he thought, although he was very aware of the smooth warmth of her skin, of how close his lips were to hers.

Instinctively, Ellie closed her eyes as the faint roughness of his skin grazed tantalisingly against hers and she felt his mouth brush the edge of her lips. It was nothing, just a brief, brotherly kiss, but it was enough to make the ground drop away beneath her feet, sending her heart lurching into her throat and leaving her giddy and aching with awareness.

And then Jack was straightening, dropping her hand, stepping away from her almost abruptly, as if even that brief physical contact had been too much for him. Convinced that even that most fleeting of kisses had reminded him bitterly of Pippa, Ellie flinched inwardly. She couldn't bear to look at him in case she saw the effort he must be making to disguise how he felt having to kiss her when he was still so in love with Alice's mother.

Hugging her arms together, she avoided Jack's eye and stood tensely by the verandah rail, watching Alice, who was happily oblivious to the sacrifices her father was making for her sake. Mug clutched in one fat little hand, she was stuffing a much-battered soft toy into her mouth with the other and talking rather indistinctly to herself.

'Well.' Jack picked up his beer and then put it down again. He felt ridiculously awkward, and he eyed Ellie uneasily. It was just as well he had only tried a peck on the cheek. There was obviously only one man she wanted to kiss her, and clearly it wasn't him.

'Well,' he said again, hating the forced heartiness in his voice, 'when shall we get married?'

'As soon as we can organise it.' Ellie strove to sound natural but couldn't quite carry it off. 'Unless you'd rather wait?' she added with stilted politeness.

Jack shook his head. 'Let's get it over and done with as soon as possible.'

He had spoken without thinking, but when he glanced down at Ellie he surprised an expression in her eyes that made him wish he had chosen his words more carefully, and he winced inwardly at his lack of tact. Their marriage might be a matter of convenience for both of them, but there had been no need to make it quite so obvious that he was dreading the wedding.

'I guess you'd rather have a quiet wedding?' he said, to break the constrained silence.

'I would, but I'm afraid we'll never get away with it.' A little colour had come back into Ellie's cheeks, and she was able to look at him almost naturally. 'You know what Mum and Lizzy are like. They'd never forgive me if we didn't have a proper wedding, and if we just go off by ourselves they'll wonder why.'

She hesitated. 'I don't want them to know why we're getting married. They'd be terribly upset if they knew the truth. Lizzy's going to be difficult enough to convince as it is. She knows how you feel about Pippa and I think she'd do everything she could to dissuade me from this if she thought we weren't going to have a genuine marriage.'

'You're probably right,' Jack agreed slowly. He and Lizzy had been friends a long time, and if anyone was going to guess that he and Ellie weren't a normal happy couple it would be her. He looked at Ellie. 'We'll have to pretend that we're in love.'

She coloured. 'Would you mind?' she asked awkwardly. 'I...I know how difficult it would be for you.'

'And for you,' he pointed out.

There was a tiny silence. Ellie couldn't look at Jack. He wasn't to know that the hardest thing for her would be to pretend that she was just pretending.

'It would only really be for the wedding,' she said, unsure whether she was reassuring him or herself.

Jack's eyes rested on her profile. 'I think I could manage that,' he said. 'If you can.'

The question in his voice made Ellie glance at him sharply. He was watching her with an unfathomable expression in his brown eyes, and when she would have looked away again she found her gaze trapped. She couldn't speak, couldn't move, could only stand and look helplessly back at him, while her heart boomed into the suddenly charged silence, so loud that she was sure that Jack must be able to hear it.

He knew, she thought in sudden panic. How could he not know when the truth of how she felt about him must be written all over her face? What if that odd expression in his eyes was really embarrassment? Or, worse, pity?

With an enormous effort, Ellie wrenched her eyes away and moistened her lips. 'I...I'll try,' she said, hating the huskiness in her voice.

'Ellie,' Jack began abruptly, then stopped, as if unsure how to continue.

Oh, God, he was going to tell her that he had guessed! Ellie steeled herself for his awkward kindness as he explained that there was no point in her hoping, but before he could finish Alice threw her mug across the verandah with a shout of triumph that made them both jump as if a gun had gone off.

Trembling, intensely grateful for the reprieve and for

the excuse to hide her face, Ellie bent to retrieve the mug and took her time about placing it very carefully on the folding table.

By the time she straightened, Jack had scooped his daughter up into his arms. 'What do you think you're doing, young lady?' he demanded with mock sternness that didn't fool Alice one bit. Beaming with satisfaction, she tugged at his hair and squealed with laughter when Jack yelped in pain.

'Hey!' he complained, tickling her in revenge, which only made Alice laugh louder.

He looked so normal that Ellie began to wonder whether she had imagined the intense look that had passed between them. He certainly couldn't have guessed that she was in love with him, or he wouldn't be able to stand there, holding Alice and laughing as if nothing had changed.

Legs weak with relief, Ellie sank down into one of the chairs. She was just being stupid.

She could even smile when Jack sat down beside with Alice on his knee. 'What will you tell Gray and Clare?'

Jack didn't answer immediately. 'I think I'd like to tell them the truth,' he said eventually, his eyes on Alice. 'I wouldn't want Clare to think that I'd forgotten Pippa so soon. You don't mind, do you?'

Ellie shook her head. 'Do you think she'll understand why you're getting married?'

'Clare will want what's best for Alice, and our marriage will be.' Jack sounded very positive. 'She's very nice,' he added, glancing at Ellie. 'You'll like her.'

'I think it's more important that she likes me,' said Ellie.

'She will,' he said confidently. 'It's Alice's birthday next Sunday. She's going to be one.' A momentary sadness shadowed his face at the thought of how alone Pippa must have felt only a year ago. 'She's too young to understand about birthdays, but we thought we ought to mark the day in some way. Why don't you come over to Bushman's Creek and meet Clare then?'

He smiled persuasively at Ellie. 'You could do with a break from painting. Come over for lunch.'

'All right,' said Ellie a little doubtfully. She wasn't sure that Alice's birthday was the best time for her to meet Clare. She would be thinking of Pippa more than usual on that day. Jack had told her how much Clare had done for Alice, and she couldn't be expected to welcome anyone who seemed to be trying to take the place of her beloved sister.

Ellie was very nervous as she drove to Bushman's Creek the following Sunday. Normally she never thought about what to wear, but that morning she had dithered for ages before deciding to put on her only dress in honour of the occasion, and as she drove up the long track leading to the homestead she wished that she had stuck to her jeans.

It wasn't that it wasn't a nice dress, but she always felt very self-conscious in it. Lizzy had bullied her into buying it the last time Ellie had visited her in Perth. Ellie could see that dusky red colour brought a flattering glow to her skin, but she was always fiddling with the little straps or tugging at the hem, trying to reveal a little less of herself.

'I just don't feel like *me* in it,' she had complained to Lizzy, but Lizzy had been insistent.

'It's perfect for you,' she said firmly. 'Just relax and enjoy looking feminine for a change!'

The trouble was that she couldn't relax in it, Ellie thought gloomily, rattling over the last cattle grid. It had seemed a good idea to try and look feminine and pretty for Jack that morning, but what was the point when she couldn't behave naturally? She just wasn't any good at being feminine and pretty. Jack would just laugh at her.

But when Jack came out to meet her, he didn't laugh. He stopped dead as Ellie got out of the car and his cheerful greeting died on his lips. It was Ellie and yet somehow not Ellie at all. She was wearing a simple red dress that stopped above the knee and showed off long, slender legs while the tiny straps revealed the warmth of her skin and the pure lines of her shoulders and throat.

It was only a dress, but Jack felt as if he had been poleaxed. 'Why...Ellie...' he said in a peculiar voice.

'Hello, Jack.'

Ellie swallowed and folded her arms in an instinctively defensive gesture. He was staring at her with such a strange expression that she felt acutely uncomfortable. Why had she worn this stupid dress? Why hadn't she brought a coat or a cardigan or *anything* to cover herself up?

'You look...you look so different.'

She glanced shyly down at herself. 'It's the dress.'

'Yes.' Jack pulled himself together with an effort. 'I'd forgotten you had legs,' he tried to joke, although when she stood there in the sunlight with that dress outlining every curve of her body it was hard to remember when he had felt less like joking. 'I don't think I've seen them since you were six!'

Ellie smiled weakly. 'That's just what Kevin said when he saw me this morning. Lizzy's always telling me to make more of an effort and dress up more, but I'd rather just wear my jeans. I feel funny like this,' she admitted in a burst of honesty.

Jack didn't think she looked funny. He thought she

looked beautiful. But he couldn't help wishing that she had worn her old paint-splattered jeans instead.

'You look fine,' he said, almost curtly.

It wasn't much of a greeting for the poor girl, he realised belatedly. He should have gone over to give her a welcoming hug. But the mere thought of putting his arm around her shoulders and feeling the warmth of her bare skin beneath his hand was oddly disturbing.

Jack was conscious of a small spurt of resentment. Ellie had no business changing. He wanted her to stay the same—quiet, gentle, undemanding, the way she had always been. He didn't want to be knocked off-balance just because she had put on some dress. He didn't want to have to think about her differently, and he wasn't going to! Dress or no dress, Jack told himself, she was still just Ellie, and there was absolutely no reason not to behave just as he had always done.

'Come and meet Clare,' he said instead, and turned on his heel to lead the way to the homestead before he changed his mind.

CHAPTER FOUR

CLARE wasn't at all as Ellie had imagined her. Slight and dark, she had beautiful, shining grey eyes and she wore her clothes with an effortless style that made Ellie glad she had put on a dress after all. Jack might not like it, but at least Clare did.

They found her in the kitchen where she was putting the finishing touches to a birthday cake for Alice. She looked up with a smile as Jack brought Ellie in, and put down the icing bag to greet her with a warm hug.

'I've been so looking forward to meeting you,' she said. 'Jack's told us how hard you've been working at Waverley Creek. Alice is obviously pleased to see you, too,' she added as the baby spotted Ellie with a crow of recognition.

She was ensconced in a highchair, and when they came in she was patting a piece of dough on her tray and examining her sticky fingers with interest, but the sight of Ellie with her father made her beam with pleasure.

Her brown eyes were so like Jack's and her smile was impossible to resist. Ellie didn't even try. Smiling back, she went over to drop a kiss on top of Alice's head, and smoothed down the fine blond hair that was just beginning to grow into wayward curls in an unthinkingly tender gesture.

She was still smiling as she glanced up to see Clare and Jack watching her. Clare was smiling, too, a little sadly, but Jack's expression was shuttered, almost unfriendly, and he turned away as if irritated by the sight of her with his daughter.

'I'll go and give Gray a hand with the barbecue,' he muttered, and strode out.

Clare saw the flash of hurt in Ellie's eyes, but she made no comment, breaking the strained silence that followed Jack's departure with a compliment about her dress instead. 'It's a fabulous colour.'

Ellie forced an answering smile. 'I'm not used to wearing dresses. Jack hardly recognised me with legs.'

She kept her voice determinedly light, but she was hurt and puzzled by Jack's behaviour. He obviously hated her dress. She could sense his discomfort, how careful he had been not to touch her and how quick to leave her.

He had looked at her as if he didn't like her. Jack had never looked at her like that before. Ellie stroked Alice's curls and fretted inwardly. It wasn't like him to be rude. Perhaps he was ill? A cold hand clutched at her heart. Perhaps he had changed his mind? Or perhaps she had said or done something to irritate him?

But what? All she had done was put on a dress! Jack was a practised charmer, always ready with the most outrageous compliments to melt the dourest of hearts. *You look fine.* That was the best he could manage for *her*!

'Sit down.' Clare appeared not to notice Ellie's struggle between hurt, concern and a stirring resentment. She picked up her icing bag once more. 'You don't mind if I finish this, do you?'

'Of course not.' Ellie made an effort to pull herself together and sat down at the table where she had sat with Lizzy what seemed like a lifetime ago.

'I'm so glad I've met you at last,' Clare was saying. 'I've heard lots about you from Jack, of course, and from Lizzy.'

Banishing Jack and his odd behaviour from her mind, Ellie gave Clare her attention. 'I'd forgotten that you knew Lizzy.'

'I was terribly jealous when I first met her,' Clare admitted. 'I knew she'd been engaged to Gray at one time, and she's so nice and such fun that I thought he was bound to be still in love with her. I was determined to dislike her, but I just couldn't!'

Ellie's face relaxed into a genuine smile. 'No, it's hard not to like Lizzy!'

'She's been a wonderful friend to Gray and to Jack, and to me,' said Clare seriously. She looked at Ellie with open interest. 'You don't look at all like her, do you?'

'No, we've always been quite different. Most people find it hard to believe that we're related at all.' Ellie sighed a little, remembering Lizzy's blond vivacity, her sparkling blue eyes and the warm charm that swept all before it. She loved Lizzy dearly, but it hadn't always been easy trailing along unnoticed in her shadow.

'Pippa and I were like that,' said Clare, to her surprise, and when Ellie looked at her she saw that there was understanding in the frank grey eyes. 'I was quiet and sensible, and she was the bright, bubbly one. She was always so full of life, so passionate about everything she did.' Her smile twisted slightly. 'There were no half-measures with Pippa.'

'I'm sorry,' said Ellie quietly. 'You must miss her very much.'

'Yes, I do.' Clare went back to her icing. 'But not all the time, not now. It was awful when she died, and for a time I thought I'd never be happy again, but I am, happier than I would have believed possible.'

She glanced at Ellie as she spoke, grey eyes shining with the thought of the love that she had found. 'It's a terrible cliché, but life really does go on. I think of Pippa often, but I don't see her ghost everywhere.'

'Jack does.' Ellie's head was bent, and she was apparently concentrating hard on drawing together a few stray crumbs on the table.

'He does at the moment, but he won't always.' Clare hesitated, picking her words with care. 'It's difficult for him being at Bushman's Creek. This is the only place he ever knew Pippa. It's full of memories of the time they spent together. It'll be different when he's at Waverley,' she added gently.

'Did...did he tell you about the arrangement we've made?'

Clare nodded. 'Yes, he did.'

'Do you mind?'

'Mind? No. I am a bit worried, though. From Jack's point of view, I can see that marriage makes sense. He needs a wife, and Alice needs a mother.'

'Are you worried that I won't look after Alice properly?' Ellie made herself ask, but Clare seemed genuinely appalled at the idea.

'Of course not! No, I'm worried about you.'

'Me?'

She hesitated. 'It's a very risky thing to marry without love. I know. It's what Gray and I did.'

'But you're happy!'

'We are now, but we weren't when we were first married. I didn't know that Gray loved me then, and he had no idea that I was desperately, desperately in love with him. We both believed that the other one just thought of our marriage as a temporary measure until Jack came home. I know how hard it can be to live with someone when you think they don't love you.'

'It's different for Jack and I,' said Ellie, still busy tidying up crumbs. 'I *know* Jack doesn't love me. He's still in love with Pippa.'

'Jack told us that you were in love with someone as well,' said Clare.

'Yes,' said Ellie dully.

There was a pause. 'It's Jack, isn't it?'

Ellie froze. She stared down at her fingers on the table, and with an odd, detached part of her mind found herself noticing a knot in the pine so intensely that afterwards she could have drawn it in exact detail.

Very slowly, she looked up to see compassion in Clare's grey gaze and knew that there was no point in denying it. 'How did you guess?'

'It was just something about the way you looked at him, something in your voice when you said his name. Don't worry, it's not that obvious. Maybe it's because I'm so in love myself that I'm more attuned to recognise it in others now.' Clare smiled a little. 'I think I used to look at Gray like that when he wasn't watching me. I know what it's like,' she added gently.

Ellie swallowed. 'You won't tell Jack, will you?' she begged, green eyes pleading.

'Of course not,' Clare reassured her. 'That's something only you can tell him.'

'I'm not going to do that,' said Ellie in a flat voice. 'Jack's only marrying me because he thinks that I'm in love with another man and won't expect anything from him that he can't give. He doesn't want anyone to take Pippa's place, and I'm not even going to try.'

'Ellie, Pippa wouldn't have wanted Jack to spend the rest of his life grieving for her,' said Clare. She had finished the cake and was sliding it carefully onto a plate. 'He won't ever forget her, but he will fall in love again. Pippa was wonderful, and I think he was very much in love with her, but that doesn't necessarily mean that they would always have been happy together.'

Straightening, she wiped her hands on her apron with a thoughtful expression. 'Pippa had a very strong personality, just like Jack. Maybe they were too alike. It would never have been a restful relationship, that's for sure.' She sighed a little. 'Who knows how long it would have lasted once the first fire and passion was over and they had to get on with the nitty-gritty of living together permanently?

'Jack will wonder that, too, sooner or later,' Clare went on. 'He's still a young man. Of course he'll get over Pippa and fall in love again, but…'

She hesitated, wondering how best to put it, and in the end it was Ellie who finished for her. 'But it won't be with me?'

'It might not be, Ellie. I wouldn't want you to build up your hopes and then be hurt. I think you'd be good for him, but we don't always fall in love with the people who'd be good for us.'

'I know that,' said Ellie with a trace of bitterness. 'If we did, I wouldn't be in love with Jack, but I am and I just have to live with it. I've faced the fact that he may fall in love with someone else eventually, and if he does, I'll let him go. He'll never know how I feel.'

'It'll be very hard, Ellie,' said Clare quietly. 'Are you sure you want to marry Jack, knowing that he doesn't love you?'

'I'm sure,' she said. 'It's my only chance to be with him, and I have to take it.'

Clare nodded, as if she had known all along that Ellie would say that. 'I hope it works out for you, Ellie. I really do.'

'I'm glad you don't mind,' said Ellie in a low voice.

'Of course I don't.' Clare smiled as she pulled off her apron and went over to wipe Alice's hands and face. 'I do feel sad about not being able to spend so much time with Alice, though. Gray and I are going to miss her horribly, but she needs to go with Jack and with you and be part of a family. Besides,' she went on with a sudden smile that lit her face, 'we're having a baby of our own. Having brought Alice up so far, I know I won't have too much time for feeling sad.'

'Oh, Clare, that's wonderful news!'

Clare laughed. 'We think so. Gray's beside himself. You'd think that no one had ever been a father before!' She lifted Alice out of the highchair and kissed her. 'We'll still miss you, though,' she promised.

Glancing at Ellie, she held the baby out to her. 'Will you take Alice?' she asked.

'Of course I will,' said Ellie, and Clare handed Alice over in a gesture that they both recognised as symbolic, although neither said anything. Ellie cuddled Alice's warm, solid little body and her eyes met Clare's in a moment of complete understanding.

Clare smiled. 'Come on,' she said. 'Let's go and find the others.'

Carrying Alice, Ellie followed Clare out to the garden at the back of the homestead, where Jack and Gray were standing in the time-honoured male position by the barbecue. They both looked round at the sound of the screen door.

Gray was a browner, quieter version of Jack, with a slow smile and an air of calm competence, but at the sight of his wife it seemed to Ellie that something lit up inside him. He didn't say anything, he didn't move, he just looked at Clare, and she looked back at him, and they might as well have kissed.

Ellie's throat tightened painfully and she felt ridiculously close to tears. If only Jack would look at her like that one day! But when she glanced at him he was just standing there with the barbecue tongs in his hand, his face empty of all expression.

Jack saw the longing in Ellie's eyes as she watched the exchange of looks between Clare and his brother, and he knew exactly what she was thinking about. It must be hard for her to see people so obviously in love with each other when her own love was so hopeless, he tried to tell himself, but it didn't stop him feeling edgy and irritable, the way he had been feeling ever since she had got out of the car in that red dress.

It wasn't Ellie's fault that he was in a bad mood, Jack knew, but somehow it felt as if it was, and she wasn't making things any better by standing there cuddling his daughter lovingly against her and thinking about another man. When he saw her glance his way, he jerked his eyes away and turned back to the barbecue to turn the steaks with a sort of controlled savagery.

'Hello, Ellie!' Gray's smile held surprise as well as pleasure as he spotted Ellie behind Clare. 'It must be years since I've seen you. You've turned into a beauty!' he teased her as he came forward to give her a hug.

Jack jabbed at the steaks. He didn't want Ellie to have turned into anything. He wanted her to stay exactly the way she had always been.

Out of the corner of his eye, he could see Ellie smiling back at Gray, shifting Alice onto her hip so that she could return his hug. He could have hugged her like that, if he hadn't been so thrown by that dress.

'I'm sorry I missed your wedding,' she was saying to Gray. 'And now I understand more congratulations are in order?' she added with a demure smile that had Jack hunching a shoulder angrily.

Where had she learnt all these feminine tricks? he wondered sourly. Put on a dress and she was suddenly Mata Hari! Where was the tomboy who had scrubbed floors on her knees and slapped paint onto walls with never a thought to her appearance?

Gray was doing a very bad job of concealing his delight. 'I've just been boasting about it to Jack,' he grinned. 'He's been longing for you to come out and rescue him.'

Ellie shot a quick glance at Jack, who was still scowling down at the barbecue. He didn't look as if he had been longing for her to come anywhere. He looked as if he wished she would go away as soon as possible.

Suppressing a sigh, she turned back to Gray and Clare. 'I'm so pleased for you,' she said honestly. 'It'll be lovely for Alice to have a cousin.' She tickled Alice's nose. 'Won't it?'

'Gah!' said Alice, so clear and unqualified a 'yes' that they couldn't help laughing.

It was Alice's day. She was too young to appreciate that it was her birthday, but she knew that the four people who meant the most to her were with her and she revelled in all the attention, showing off shamelessly. She had a whole piece of the chocolate cake that Clare had made, and showed her appreciation by sticking her fingers in it and proceeding to wipe them over her face and hair before sucking them with noisy relish.

Jack's ill-humour dissolved as he watched her. It was impossible to stay cross when Alice was peeping glances under her lashes with mischievous brown eyes, when she crowed with delighted laughter or tried to imitate Ellie

clapping but couldn't quite manage to bring her choco-
latey hands together at the same time.

He would do anything for her, Jack vowed. She was
the reason that he was marrying Ellie. What did it matter
if Ellie was in love with someone else as long as she was
there for Alice?

He slid a sideways glance at Ellie. She was relaxed in
her chair, laughing at Alice's antics, glowing in the red
dress, her awkwardness forgotten. Jack felt something
shift in his chest, and he looked quickly away.

Later, when Alice was asleep, exhausted by all the
excitement, he walked Ellie to her car.

'I'm sorry I haven't been much company today,' he
said abruptly, breaking the constrained silence between
them.

'That's all right,' said Ellie. 'I realised that you were
thinking of Pippa.' She hesitated. 'It must have been a
difficult day for you.'

'It wasn't that,' he said honestly. 'I have been thinking
of her, of course, but... I don't know what it was,' he
confessed with a sigh. 'Maybe the whole idea just takes
some getting used to.'

He glanced down at Ellie. Her lashes were lowered,
guarding her expression, and it occurred to him that for
all her familiarity there was something elusive about her.
He had always thought of Ellie as being quiet and
straightforward, but the more he saw of her, the more
mysterious she seemed.

'We've got over the first hurdle anyway,' he said,
striving for a lighter tone. 'I wasn't looking forward to
telling Clare that I was marrying you, but she seems to
approve. Now we just need to convince your family.
Have you told them yet?'

'Yes.'

'How did they take it?'

'Mum's over the moon, and is already deep in plans for the wedding. Dad doesn't say very much, but I think he's pleased. Kevin and Sue were even more pleased—I think they were relieved to hear that I wasn't planning on staying with them for ever!'

'And Lizzy?'

She grimaced. 'Lizzy's suspicious,' she admitted. 'She knows how you feel about Pippa, and she knows me. She guessed the truth right away.'

Jack glanced at her. 'The truth?' he said, an odd inflection in his voice, and she stopped by the car to look at him in surprise.

'That you're just looking for a mother for Alice.'

'Did she guess the truth about you, too?'

Ellie's eyes shifted. 'She thinks I'll do anything to stay in the outback. I didn't tell her…anything else.'

'So did you tell her that she guessed right?'

'No.' Ellie shrugged, as if trying to shake off an uncomfortable memory. 'I don't like lying to her, but you know how romantic she is about marriage. She thinks that you should only get married if you're passionately in love and everything's perfect. I had to pretend that that's how it is for us.'

Jack leant against the bonnet of the car and folded his arms. 'Did she believe you?'

'I'm not sure.' Ellie bit her lip. 'I don't think so, not really. She asked when it had all happened, of course, and I said that we'd got to know each other better while I was helping you at Waverley, but that wasn't enough for Lizzy!'

Her eyes kindled with remembered indignation at the interrogation Lizzy had put her through. 'She wanted to know every detail!'

Jack could imagine Lizzy's reaction to Ellie's carefully understated story only too well, and swift amusement gleamed in his brown eyes. 'What sort of detail?' he asked.

'Oh, you know…' Ellie's gaze slid away from his, and she rested her hand against the car door, running her finger down the windowframe. 'How we fell in love. When we first kissed. What it was like. That kind of thing.'

'What did you say?'

When she risked a fleeting glance at him, she saw with a trace of resentment that there was still a smile lurking at the back of his eyes. It was all very well for him to find it funny. *He* hadn't had Lizzy on the phone for hours, asking awkward questions she couldn't answer.

'What about?' she asked almost snappishly.

'About our first kiss.'

'I said it was wonderful, of course,' said Ellie crossly. 'I couldn't very well say that I'd never kissed you, could I?'

'Not if you want her to believe that we're passionately in love,' agreed Jack.

'She says she's coming home from Perth next weekend to see for herself,' Ellie went on glumly. 'She's already asked Mum and Dad what they're doing about an engagement party. I tried to tell them that we were too busy at Waverley for a party, but I might as well have spared my breath! They're busy inviting half the district. Just because they love parties doesn't mean I do! Why can't they leave us alone?' she demanded wildly.

'Poor Ellie!' Jack couldn't help laughing at her expression. 'They just want to make things special for you. It won't be that bad.'

Ellie refused to be consoled. 'Yes, it will. It'll be *awful*. I won't be able to relax for a minute. Everyone will be there, looking at me, and Lizzy will be watching us like a hawk to see if we really are in love or not.'

Jack unfolded his arms and straightened from the bonnet. 'We'll just have to be ready to put on a convincing show, then, won't we?' he said.

'How are we supposed to do that?' she asked, still preoccupied by her grievance over the party.

'Well...' Jack pretended to consider the matter. 'We could kiss,' he suggested casually.

'K-kiss?' stammered Ellie, jerked out of her abstraction.

'It's usual at engagement parties, especially when you're the couple getting engaged.'

'I know, but...'

'It's not a problem, is it?'

She swallowed. 'No...no... At least...' She trailed off incoherently, unable to explain to Jack why the thought of kissing him threw her into such confusion.

'If it is, perhaps we should practise now,' said Jack, as if struck by a sudden thought.

'Practise?' she croaked.

'I'm going to have to kiss you at the party, and at the wedding,' he pointed out. 'I just thought it might be a good idea if I kissed you now so that it doesn't look as if it's our first time when we have to do it in front of everyone else.'

He made it sound so normal, so obvious, as if it would mean no more than shaking hands. 'What do you think?' he asked.

His face was perfectly straight, but there was a deepening of the creases around his eyes, a suspicion of a smile lurking around his mouth. Ellie didn't know at that moment whether she loved him or hated him for finding the idea of kissing her so amusing.

'I...don't know,' she said stiffly.

'At least then if anyone else asks you what our first kiss was like you'll be able to tell them.'

Her heart was slamming in slow, painful strokes against her ribs and her throat was so tight that she could hardly breathe. She stared uncertainly at Jack, half afraid that he would turn out to be joking after all. She longed to kiss him, but dreaded it at the same time, terrified of what she would reveal if she did.

'I won't kiss you if you don't want me to,' said Jack softly, and when she still said nothing, he made as if to step away.

'No,' said Ellie involuntarily, and he stopped, lifting his eyebrows. She had longed for this moment for years. How could she run away from it now?

'I mean...no, I think you're right,' she managed to croak as she struggled for composure. 'It's a good idea.'

It *was*, she told herself. If she was going to make a fool out of herself, it was far better to do it now, alone with Jack in the yard at Bushman's Creek, than at some party with the entire district looking on.

'We...we don't want to look silly at the party, do we?' she went on, mustering a brave smile from somewhere.

'No,' Jack agreed slowly.

The lurking smile evaporated from his eyes. Ellie's grumbling about the party had been reassuringly familiar, her awkwardness about the idea of kissing him endearing, reminding him that this was the same, safe Ellie he had always known and not some stranger in a red dress.

But now he was going to kiss her, and his indulgent amusement evaporated as they looked at each other in strumming silence. Jack felt absurdly nervous. He had kissed lots of women, but not like Ellie. Ellie was different.

He took her by the waist as hesitantly as the first time he had ever kissed a girl. He could feel the warmth of her body, the slight shift of her dress beneath his palms, the cool, smooth material slipping over her bare skin, and his throat dried.

Ellie was trembling. Her pulse boomed in her ears and her legs seemed to have disappeared so that the burning touch of his hands through her dress seemed to be all that was keeping her upright.

She had to help him. Desperately she tried to steady her spinning senses. It couldn't be easy for Jack to kiss her. She had felt his hesitation and knew that he must be thinking of Pippa, the only girl he really wanted to kiss.

Taking a deep breath, she put her hands on his shoulders. Beneath her wondering fingers, his shirt was soft over steel-hard muscles.

She had loved Jack for his reckless charm, for the faint, indefinable sense of danger that edged his lazy good humour and his kindness, for the warmth of his eyes and the way the sun rose when he smiled, but in that moment she was conscious only of him as a man.

She wanted to slide her hands beneath his shirt and spread her fingers over his bare chest. She wanted to explore the hardness of his body and burrow into his lean strength. Physical desire churned through her, leaving her sick and giddy and so afraid that she would simply succumb to it that she was about to step back when Jack pulled her closer and her last hope of resistance had gone.

Tightening one arm around her, he lifted the other hand to smooth the hair from her face before letting it slide down her throat so that he could caress the line of her jaw almost absently with his thumb.

Ellie stood stock-still, staring blindly at the pulse that beat steadily below his ear, quivering at the merest graze of his fingers against her cheek. She knew that she was lost.

'Look at me, Ellie,' said Jack, his voice so deep that it seemed to vibrate through her.

Slowly, unresistingly, Ellie lifted her eyes, and the breath snared in her throat. Jack was looking down into her face with an unfathomable expression, but his hand was sliding beneath her hair, holding her still at the nape of her neck, and anticipation shivered over her skin.

And then the long waiting was over and he was bending his head, and Ellie had time only to sweep her lashes over her eyes before his mouth came down on hers. It was a very gentle kiss, but the mere touch of his lips sent such a jolt of response through her that she gasped and her fingers curled instinctively into his shirt. When he lifted his head almost immediately she had to struggle not to cry out in protest.

So that was it. Disappointment gripped Ellie by the throat. Swallowing, she opened her eyes, but she couldn't have said anything if she had tried. She didn't know any tricks, any little way of letting him know how desperately she wanted him to kiss her again. She could only stare dumbly back at him.

Jack had meant to let her go at once. She hadn't wanted to kiss him, not really, he remembered. A brief kiss would have been enough. But the piercing sweetness of her lips had caught him unawares, and somehow, instead of releasing her as he'd intended, he found his arm sliding round to gather her closer, and before he knew quite was happening he was lifting her up to kiss her again, the way a girl in a red dress should be kissed.

Delight mingled with relief cascaded through her in a tumbling golden rush, and she melted into him, beyond fear that she would give herself away, beyond worry about the complications of their situation, beyond thinking about anything but Jack, the taste of him and the feel of him and the glorious knowledge that she was in his arms at last.

Her hands crept up from his shoulders to wind around his neck, and she abandoned herself to the honeyed pleasure spilling along her veins. His mouth, moving so warm and persuasive against hers, was intoxicating, the strength of the arm that held her fast encircled her with enchantment.

It didn't matter to Ellie that there were no stars, no romantic backdrop to their first kiss. She didn't care that she was standing in a dusty yard sheltered only by the straggly shade of a gum, that Jack had ignored her for most of the day, or that the kiss meant no more to him than an amusing rehearsal. She cared only that it was her turn, that his arms were around *her*, that his lips were on hers.

Ellie never knew how long the kiss lasted. It might have been a few seconds; it might have been an hour. All she knew was that it ended much too soon. When Jack let her go, she leant shakily back against the car door, heedless of the handle digging into her back, boneless and trembling. The world was still rocking around her and she had to lay her hands flat against the hot metal to steady herself.

Jack was the first to recover. 'Do you think that would have convinced Lizzy?' he asked, and although he tried to sound unconcerned he could hear the ragged edge to his voice.

'I hope so,' said Ellie huskily. It had nearly convinced her.

Unable to meet Jack's eyes, she fumbled for the door handle behind her. 'I...I'd better go,' she managed.

Jack watched as she scrambled into the driving seat and bent to insert the key with fingers that felt thick and clumsy. The sweetness of her kiss had caught him unawares, and his senses strummed with a new and disconcerting awareness of the softness of her lips, the pliancy of her body, the scent of her skin.

He had wanted to kiss her again, but her eyes had held a stricken expression and she had turned away so quickly that for the first time ever Jack wondered if she had enjoyed the kiss at all. She obviously couldn't wait to close the door between them and get away.

Acutely conscious of his gaze on her, Ellie became more and more flustered. It took ages to get the key in the ignition, but at last it slotted into place and she braced herself to look at him, certain that he would be laughing at her confusion.

But Jack wasn't laughing. He was just watching her with a faintly worried expression in his brown eyes. It lightened slightly as she wound down the window to say goodbye.

'You'll tell Gray and Clare about the party?' she said with stilted politeness.

'Of course,' said Jack, equally formal.

He hesitated, concerned by the paleness of her face, the over-brightness of her smile, the way she clutched at the steering wheel as if for support. 'Are you all right, Ellie?' he asked in a different tone, putting out a hand to rest on the open window.

'I'm fine.'

'You didn't mind me kissing you?'

'Of course not,' said Ellie with an unconvincing smile. 'It's me that wants to convince my family that we're in love. That was part of the deal.'

The deal. The reason they were getting married. The

reason she was there. The reason he had forgotten when he was kissing her.

'Oh, yes, the deal,' said Jack in a flat voice, and he stepped back from the car to let her go.

CHAPTER FIVE

JACK didn't want to go to any engagement party the following weekend. Especially not his own.

He had been in a bad mood all week. It was his own fault for kissing Ellie, of course. Jack knew that. It had seemed like a good idea at the time, but he hadn't bargained for the way the memory would stick like a burr in his mind.

He was disconcerted to find himself thinking about Ellie at odd times of the day. About the way she had looked in that dress, about the slender smoothness of her legs and the unexpected sweetness of her lips, and sometimes his palm would tingle as if he could still feel the silkiness of her dress slipping over her skin.

Whenever that happened, Jack would shrug the memory aside. It had only been Ellie, he reminded himself at rather too frequent intervals. He had kissed much prettier girls much more passionately. There was no reason for that particular kiss to leave him feeling restless and uneasy.

It wasn't even as if Ellie herself had been bothered by it. It had been part of the deal, as she had pointed out, and it annoyed Jack that he couldn't forget it as easily as she apparently had.

He was silent as they drove to the party, content to let Gray and Clare talk in the front while he sat in the back next to Alice. Firmly strapped into her car seat, she amused herself by playing with her toes until the monotonous vibration of the car lulled her to sleep.

Jack's eyes rested on her as her head lolled at an awkward angle onto her shoulder. Her mouth was slightly open, and the ridiculously long lashes fanned her rosy cheeks. Unsettled and out of humour, he had been on the point of ringing Ellie to cancel their engagement several times during the past week, but whenever he'd picked up the phone he had thought of Alice.

Alice, who was Pippa's daughter. Alice, who needed a mother. It was for her that he was marrying Ellie.

No, he reassured himself as he watched his daughter sleeping, he was doing the right thing. He just wished that he hadn't spoilt everything by kissing Ellie.

Jack was irritatingly aware that, in spite of all his misgivings, he was looking forward to seeing her again. It wasn't supposed to be like this, he thought crossly as Gray turned onto the sealed road. The idea had been that Ellie would be a gentle, undemanding friend, a restful companion, someone who would be there when he needed her but who he wouldn't really need to think about the rest of the time.

Jack scowled out of the car window. Ellie wasn't supposed to put on red dresses and confuse him like this.

His mood was not improved when they arrived at the party to find Ellie wearing the same damned dress and looking even prettier than he had remembered. She was giving an incredibly convincing performance of a girl happily in love, Jack noted with an obscure sense of resentment.

He should have been grateful to her for carrying off the pretence so well, but somehow he wasn't. He didn't like the way her eyes sparkled as she talked and laughed. He didn't like the way the men she had known all her life clustered around her. He didn't like the way they looked at her.

Jack glowered as he watched Ellie. He didn't have to be told that the man she loved was there. There was a glow about her today, and it certainly wasn't for him. He found himself studying the face of every man there, wondering which of them was responsible for her radiance.

She ought to have more pride, Jack decided austerely. She had told him that she had given up hope of having her love returned, but why else would she be smiling like that? Why else would she be wearing that red dress like that?

Across the room, Ellie saw the compressed line of Jack's mouth and suppressed a sigh. She had been horribly nervous about seeing him again after that kiss, hiding her apprehension behind an air of desperate gaiety.

It was very important that Jack should have no inkling of what his kiss had meant to her. He would be appalled if he knew how she had lain awake every night since then, reliving every second, remembered pleasure shuddering slowly down her spine

From the moment he had walked into the party it had been obvious that Jack's feelings were very different. Ellie had seen from his face how much he regretted kissing her, and guessed that he was terrified in case she had misinterpreted it.

Well, he needn't worry, thought Ellie, lifting her chin proudly. She had no intention of embarrassing him or of making a fuss.

She smiled brightly at Jack to reassure him, but he didn't respond. He managed a smile for her parents, but couldn't wait to get away and join the massed ranks of his ex-girlfriends, who were all eagerly awaiting the chance to greet him. He managed to smile at them, too, Ellie noted sourly, watching as he returned their hugs with unnecessary warmth.

As the party wore on, and Jack continued to avoid her, Ellie began to get cross. It wasn't her fault Jack had kissed her! If he didn't want to marry her, he could have said. He needn't have come today at all, but, since he had, he could at least make the effort to behave like a fiancé.

As it was, she was left pretending to be engaged single-handed! Uncomfortably aware of how much effort her family were making for her, Ellie resisted the temptation to march over to Jack, slap all those girls' hands off his arm and tell him he could look elsewhere for an unpaid housekeeper if that was all he wanted. Her parents were so delighted for her that she couldn't bear to disappoint them by letting her feelings show. They wanted her to have a wonderful time, and a wonderful time she would seem to be having!

Ellie put up her chin and fixed a glittering smile to her face. Jack could make it obvious that he wasn't in love with her if he wanted, but she would play the part of a deliriously happy fiancée if it killed her!

She had known almost everyone at the party her entire life, so it wasn't that difficult to enjoy herself—or it wouldn't have been if she could have ignored Jack as comprehensively as he was ignoring her. But whenever she looked at him he had some other girl hanging around him. They were all blond, all pretty, and Ellie was prepared to bet that they all knew just as well as her what it felt like to be kissed by Jack.

A sudden sense of hopelessness swept over her. Who was she trying to fool? It must be obvious to anyone with eyes in their head that she wasn't Jack's type. Did anyone in this room really believe that out of all the girls there who would have jumped at the chance of marrying Jack he had chosen her, quiet, ordinary Ellie Walker?

Of course not.

Ellie's carefully bright smile slipped from her face. All at once she felt exposed and humiliated, as if the entire room were sniggering behind their hands at her pathetic attempts to catch Jack for herself when he so obviously belonged with someone pretty and clever and fun. Someone unlike her.

She had to get away. Murmuring an excuse, Ellie glanced around her to make sure that no one noticed where she was going and slipped out of the room. From the kitchen she could hear the sound of cheerful voices as her mother and her friends prepared endless salads for the evening meal, and she turned the other way, escaping instinctively to the far corner of the back verandah, where she could hide behind the potted palms that helped keep the shade cool and green.

Ellie sank gratefully down into one of the old wicker chairs. The effort of smiling for so long had taken its toll, and she rubbed her aching jaw, savouring the silence and the blessed relief of being on her own.

'What are you doing out here?'

Ellie's head jerked up at the sound of Jack's voice. He was striding down the verandah towards her with a thunderous expression, and her stomach gave a great lurch that was partly shock, partly anger, partly exasperation with herself for loving him even when he was being cross and unreasonable.

'What does it look like I'm doing?' she retorted, thrown off-balance by his obvious fury. What did *he* have to be so angry about?

'Meeting this famous lover of yours?' Jack suggested in a deliberately offensive voice.

Ellie was so taken aback that she could only stare at him. 'What?'

'I saw you look around to check that no one was watching you before sneaking off,' he told her. 'It was perfectly obvious that you were going off to meet someone. I thought you told me there was nothing between you?'

'There isn't,' she said tightly, torn between relief that he hadn't, after all, guessed how she felt, and anger at his sheer obtuseness.

'Oh?' Jack didn't even bother to hide his disbelief. 'Then what were you doing sneaking out of the room like that?'

'I wasn't *sneaking*! I needed some air, and I just wanted to be on my own for a bit. I didn't want anyone to follow me,' she added pointedly, but Jack refused to take the hint.

He threw himself down in the chair next to hers and eyed her moodily. 'Why not?'

'I don't like parties.'

'You could have fooled me,' said Jack. 'I would have said that you were having a wonderful time in there.'

Ellie drew in a sharp breath. 'Why would I have been having a good time, Jack?' she asked, dangerously quiet. 'I've had to spend the day lying to my family and friends. I've had to pretend to be happily engaged to a man who's spent the entire time ignoring me. I've had to put up with pitying looks from all your ex-girlfriends, who are plainly wondering why on earth you're marrying me when you're clearly not in the slightest bit interested in me. What makes you think that I've been enjoying that?'

Jack scowled. 'I haven't been ignoring you. I just haven't been able to get near you all day. Whenever I saw you, you seemed more than happy to be the centre of attention.'

'It's called making an effort,' snapped Ellie. 'Mum and

Dad have gone to a lot of trouble to arrange this party for us, and they'd be really upset if they thought I was less than deliriously happy. Of *course* I've been looking as if I'm having a good time! What do you expect me to do? Stand there looking miserable?'

'Flirting with every man in sight seems a funny way of convincing your parents that you're happily engaged,' said Jack unpleasantly.

It was so unfair that Ellie was momentarily deprived of breath. *'Flirting?'* she gasped as she stared at him in gathering fury. 'I haven't been flirting with anyone! I wouldn't even know *how* to flirt!'

'Oh, I wouldn't say that,' he sneered. 'In fact, I'd say you had that wide-eyed, artless look down to a fine art! And nobody could say that you were picking on anyone in particular, which I'm sure was your object. I must be the only man here you *didn't* flirt with!'

'I might have done if you'd come anywhere near me,' said Ellie in a shaking voice. 'You obviously had much better things to do. I'm surprised you even noticed what I was doing!'

'Of course I noticed.'

Jack glared at Ellie, but even as he glared he was disturbingly aware of her. The red dress was like a flame in the dim shade, her eyes were green with anger and she looked startlingly, even shockingly, vivid. The memory of how it had felt to kiss her caught suddenly at Jack's heart, making it stumble, and he got abruptly to his feet to prowl over to the verandah rail and stand with his back to her.

'We *are* supposed to be engaged,' he pointed out.

'Oh, so you remembered?' Ellie had never, ever quarrelled with Jack before, and the realisation that she could actually be angry with him was curiously exhilarating.

'That would explain, of course, why you've been avoiding me and paying such close attention to all your ex-girlfriends instead!'

Jack shut his teeth. 'I've just been catching up with old friends,' he said, unwilling to admit how the sight of Ellie surrounded by so many obviously admiring men had thrown him off-balance.

'Funny how all your *old friends* just happen to be young, female and very pretty!'

It wasn't like Ellie to be sarcastic, and Jack didn't like it one bit. His mouth tightened as he swung round to face her.

'Don't be ridiculous! I've talked to almost everyone here today, which is more than you have. I've been polite to your aunts, said all the right things to your father and your brother and been grilled by your mother and Lizzy. I would have talked to you, too, but I haven't been able to get near you all day. It would have meant fighting my way through the throng of men who were all anxious to get an eyeful of you in that dress!'

There was a blistering silence. They eyed each other with dislike, although both were secretly appalled at the quarrel which had sprung up between them and which had already turned nastier than either of them would have been able to imagine.

It was Jack who turned away first. 'He's here, isn't he?' he asked in a different voice.

'Who?'

'The man you're in love with.'

Ellie looked at his back and sighed. 'Yes,' she said after a moment.

'I could tell,' said Jack without looking at her. 'It's as if someone switched on a light inside you. Pippa used to look like that. She said that it was just knowing that I was near.'

Ellie didn't want to hear about Pippa. She got to her feet and went to stand next to Jack by the verandah rail, although not close enough to touch him. 'Yes, that's what it is,' she said heavily.

'Is he married? Is that the problem?'

'I don't want to talk about it.'

'Every unmarried guy in the district was panting over you in there,' Jack persisted. 'There isn't one of them who wouldn't jump at the chance of unzipping that dress. All you'd have to do is lift a finger and you could have whichever one of them you wanted, so it must be someone else.'

'Jack.' Ellie gritted her teeth and spoke very distinctly. 'I do not want to talk about it, all right?'

'I wouldn't tell anyone. I just want to know.'

'It's none of your business.'

'The hell it isn't! We're getting married!'

'We had a deal,' she said stonily. 'I told you the situation, and you said that you understood. I'm not prepared to discuss it any further.'

'And that's it?' Jack eyed her set face with a mixture of bafflement and frustration. 'I'm supposed to stand by and watch while you light up every time this guy is in the same room as you?'

It was at this inauspicious moment that the sound of high heels clicking on the wooden floor announced the arrival of Lizzy.

'There you are!' she exclaimed as she came down the verandah towards them. 'What on earth are you doing hiding out here? I've been looking for you everywhere. We want to have the toast, and Dad's going to give a speech—'

She stopped as she took in the way Jack and Ellie were standing rigidly apart, their faces set.

'Uh-oh! I smell tension in the air! What's going on?'

'Nothing,' said Ellie.

'Just a little lovers' tiff,' said Jack at the same time. He bared his teeth at Ellie. 'Isn't it, darling?'

Ellie only glared back at him, and Lizzy's mouth twitched.

'Are you planning to kiss and make up, or shall I go and tell Dad the wedding's off?' she asked, opening her eyes innocently.

'Of course the wedding's not off.' The smoothness of Jack's voice was in direct contrast to the hardness of his grip as his fingers closed around Ellie's wrist. 'You can all get your glasses ready. We're coming.'

To Lizzy's evident amusement, he practically dragged Ellie back inside. Ellie had to almost run to keep up with him, and only just remembered in time to fix a brittle smile to her face before he jerked her to a halt beside her father.

Steeling herself to meet the embarrassed stares of everyone around her, Ellie was amazed to discover that there was not a single raised eyebrow in sight, and that they were all smiling fondly as her father launched into his speech. Couldn't they *see* that Jack's smile didn't match the cold anger in his eyes? That he was holding her hand in a punishing grip? That the air between them was fairly crackling with acrimony?

Only Lizzy seemed to be aware that anything was wrong, and instead of looking concerned, she wore a pleased smile. Ellie stared suspiciously at her. Lizzy had been the only doubter when she had announced her engagement to Jack, and had been clearly reserving her

judgement until she saw the two of them together. Why,
then, was she suddenly looking so satisfied?

Ellie felt as if she had been standing there for hours
with Jack's merciless fingers around her own before her
father eventually came to the end of his speech. Everyone
laughed dutifully at his appalling jokes, and nodded sen-
timentally when he told them that Jack and Ellie were
made for each other. Ellie couldn't bear to look at Jack
then, but she felt his hand tighten so hard that she winced.

'So I'd like you all to raise your glasses—' her father
was beaming as he wound up at last '—and drink to the
future happiness of Ellie and Jack.'

'Ellie and Jack!' they all chorused obediently, raising
their glasses with such goodwill that Ellie squirmed inwardly.

The arrangement she and Jack had come to had seemed
their own business until she'd realised that it meant de-
ceiving an awful lot of people she cared about. It would
have been much easier if they had all ignored her engagement altogether, instead of overwhelming her with
their delight and good wishes.

The cheers died away, and in the expectant hush that
followed Ellie found herself the focus of all eyes. They
were waiting for Jack to kiss her.

The realisation sent the air whooshing out of Ellie's
lungs, and her bright smile faltered as she glanced nervously at Jack. He would make some excuse, she reassured herself. He couldn't possibly kiss her now, not with
their quarrel still ringing in their ears.

But when she tried to tug her hand away, Jack
wouldn't let her go. He pulled her towards him instead,
turning to look down at her with a smile that made her
insides jerk themselves into a tangled knot of apprehen-

sion and alarm, threaded through with the treacherous
pulse of excitement.

Ellie opened her mouth, although she had no idea what
she would have said, and in any case it was too late. Jack
had jerked her roughly into his arms, and his mouth came
down on hers before she had a chance to protest.

It wasn't how he had kissed her before. This time there
was no sweetness, no drench of delight. This kiss was a
challenge.

Jack's lips were fierce and demanding, his hands hard
against the bare flesh of her arms, and the anger surged
between them like an electric current. Ellie was riveted
by the intensity of her response. She could feel it rock-
eting through her, jolting, explosive, terrifyingly uncon-
trollable, and yet edged with elation.

So Jack wanted to punish her, did he? Well, she was
tired of being the dear, sweet little Ellie who would put
up with all his moods without question! If his kiss was
a challenge, she could meet it!

Curling her fingers into his shirt, defiant, even provocative, Ellie kissed Jack back. She had forgotten that they
were surrounded by people who would all be watching
them, forgotten the arrangement they had made and why
they were there. Nothing mattered but the clash of wills
and the undertow of a dark, dangerous excitement that
ran between them.

Afterwards, Ellie couldn't have said when that turbu-
lent kiss changed, but just as it seemed set to blaze out
of control the fierce antagonism vaporised into pleasure
so intense that her bones liquefied and she had to hold
more tightly on to Jack to stop herself dissolving away
altogether.

It was as if their mouths had been made to move together, urgently seeking the source of that whirling

delight, as if Jack's hands had been specially designed to slide possessively down her spine, to gather her closer, as if her body had always been meant to melt into his unyielding strength.

'Hey, break it up!' a voice somewhere called. 'There are children here!'

The burst of laughter and cheering that followed seemed to Ellie to come from a thousand miles away. It was nothing to do with her or with Jack, and when she felt him begin to draw away she murmured in instinctive protest.

Jack hesitated, then ignored it. When he lifted his head, Ellie was disorientated to find that, far from being alone, a thousand miles from anyone else, they were surrounded by grinning faces. Swallowing, she blinked back at them with dark, dazed eyes.

What had happened? One minute she and Jack had been kissing each other furiously, and the next... Ellie didn't know why it had changed or what it meant. She knew only that she felt boneless and bewildered, and so shaken that she was afraid to move in case she simply collapsed into an untidy heap on the floor. Jack's hands at her waist were all that was keeping her upright.

Almost reluctantly, her eyes met Jack's. He was looking appalled, and they stared at each other in consternation, too shocked at first to wonder what their interested audience would think. That thought occurred to them simultaneously, and as if at some unspoken signal they stepped abruptly away from each other.

For some reason, everyone seemed to find their behaviour funny. There was laughter and cheering and good-natured whistles, and then the crowd lifted their glasses again as one.

'To Jack and Ellie!'

By the time they had waved off the last of the guests that evening, Ellie was exhausted. She had somehow managed to pull herself together and continue chatting brightly, as if Jack kissed her like that every day, but she had longed for everyone to go so that she could shut herself away somewhere and stop smiling.

She and Jack were very careful not to touch again. Jack took Alice from Gray, which gave him a good excuse not to have to hold her hand or put his arm around her waist as a real lover would have done. Ellie told herself it was better that way, but it didn't stop her feeling cold and confused and very alone.

They barely spoke to each other until Jack came to say goodbye with Gray and Clare. He was still holding Alice, and Ellie was able to make a big fuss of saying goodbye to her without once meeting his eyes.

'I was thinking of going over to Waverley next week,' Jack said awkwardly. 'What about you? Are you busy?'

Ellie wasn't sure whether he wanted her to pretend that she couldn't go with him or not, but her brother and sister-in-law were standing right beside her and they knew perfectly well that she had nothing else to do. Besides, wouldn't it be better just to pretend that nothing had happened?

'No, I'll be there.' She flashed a bright, meaningless smile somewhere over his shoulder. 'I've still got those windows to finish.'

'Gray and I are mustering tomorrow and Tuesday, so I won't be going before Wednesday,' said Jack with the same stilted politeness. 'I could pick you up on the way, if you like.'

'Fine.'

Jack hesitated, as if he wanted to say something else, but in the end he just nodded. 'I'll see you then.'

Hugging her arms together, Ellie watched as he settled Alice into the car seat and got in beside her without even a glance over his shoulder to where she was standing at the bottom of the verandah steps.

Long after they had gone, she carried on standing there, looking after them, and it was only when she turned that she discovered that Lizzy was there too, eyeing her with a very strange expression.

'What?' said Ellie defensively, even though Lizzy hadn't said a word.

'I was just remembering how appalled I was when you told me you were going to marry Jack,' said Lizzy. 'I thought that you were both getting married for all the wrong reasons, and when I saw how politely you greeted each other today I was sure of it, whatever you'd told me. But as soon as I saw you quarrelling I knew that I was wrong and you were right after all.'

'You did?' Ellie looked at her sister, wondering what on earth she was talking about.

'Oh, yes.' Lizzy nodded vigorously. 'You were having a real fight when I walked in, weren't you? That's a very good sign.'

'It is?'

'Come on, Ellie, you've never fought in your life, and I don't think I've ever seen Jack lose his temper like that. He's always been so laid-back. You wouldn't have been having an argument like that unless there was something special between you. You have to care about someone a lot to argue like that—and to kiss like that,' she added as an afterthought.

She smiled a little wistfully. 'I wish I could find someone who would kiss me like that, not caring who was watching or what they were thinking. I think you're very lucky, Ellie.'

'Lizzy,' Ellie began impulsively, then stopped. She had been about to tell Lizzy the truth, that there was something between her and Jack, but not what she thought it was. It was a deal, not love. But Lizzy was looking so pleased for her that Ellie couldn't face her reaction if she knew what they had agreed. Lizzy would tell her parents, and everyone would be bitterly disappointed and hurt that Ellie had lied.

No, Ellie decided, she couldn't do it. She turned instead to look back at where the lights of the car had disappeared into darkness, taking Jack with them.

Her lips still tingled from his kiss; her body still boomed where he had held her against him. It might not be the way she had wanted, but at least she had kissed him instead of spending her life loving him from afar and wondering what it would be like.

She could have been stuck in a city job by now, Ellie reminded herself, pining for the outback. She could have been watching tonight as Jack got engaged to another girl who would be a mother for Alice. She wouldn't have to face that now. He was going to marry her, and she would be able to stay at Waverley, with him.

It wasn't everything she wanted, but it was a lot. It was enough.

'Yes,' she agreed slowly, 'I'm very lucky.'

Jack picked her up on Wednesday at first light. Ellie was waiting for him at the airstrip, and he left the propeller spinning blurrily as she climbed in beside him.

'Hello, Ellie.'

'Hi,' she said brightly, making a big fuss about fastening her belt so that she didn't have to look at him directly.

She was determined to behave naturally. Ellie had done a lot of thinking since the party. Jack's kiss was

seared on her memory, raw and disturbing. She felt sick
and shaken when she thought about how treacherously
her body had responded, but she had made up her mind.

She was going to marry Jack. Living with him was
obviously going to be more difficult than she had
thought, but it would be better than living without him.
All she had to do was pretend that nothing out of the
ordinary had happened at the party, that he had never
kissed her and that she had never kissed him back with
that aching hunger.

Easier said than done.

Ellie was agonisingly aware of Jack beside her as the
little plane sped down the airstrip and lifted into the air.
She felt the familiar drop of her stomach as the ground
fell away beneath them, the same lurch of alarm and anticipation she felt whenever she saw Jack, whenever she
thought about the way he smiled, the way he squinted
against the sun, the way he tilted his hat on his head.

Jack seemed to be absorbed in flying the plane. Ellie
took the chance to study him from under her lashes. He
sat relaxed in his seat, his hands sure and steady on the
joystick, his eyes intent as he checked the instrument
panel.

Her gaze rested on his profile. Everything about him
was so familiar: the creases at the edges of his eyes, the
angular planes of his face, the long, mobile mouth. But
now she knew how exciting those lips felt against her
own. She knew the strength of his hands and the hardness
of his body in a way she had only been able to imagine
before.

Ellie's insides clenched, remembering. Now everything was different.

CHAPTER SIX

JERKING her eyes away from Jack, she moistened her lips and sought desperately for something to say.

'D-did you bring more paint for the bathroom?' Hardly the most sparkling of conversation openers, but the best she could manage.

'Enough to do that and to finish Alice's room, too.'

Jack was intensely grateful to Ellie for breaking the uncomfortable silence. They talked decorating for a while, and when that subject was exhausted, and the silence yawned around them once more, they talked about how much rain there had been and how high the creeks were running. They were even driven to talking about fixing the generator at Waverley and how much fuel they would need to order.

Their stilted conversation filled the silence, but it didn't stop the memory of the kiss they had shared strumming in the air between them.

In the end, Jack could bear it no longer. He broke off in the middle of telling Ellie what was needed to make the stockmen's quarters habitable to say abruptly, 'I'm sorry about the other day.'

'The other day?' said Ellie, thrown by the sudden change of subject.

'I was out of order,' he said. 'You were right. Your feelings for this other man are none of my business. I never meant to quarrel with you like that,' he went on awkwardly. 'I don't know why I was so angry. It just seemed to be a difficult situation, and I guess I was on edge.'

'I think we both were,' she said, trying desperately to keep her voice light.

Jack took a breath. 'It's not just the argument. I need to apologise about that kiss, too.'

'Oh, that,' said Ellie weakly.

'I don't know what was the matter with me,' he said, determined to make a full confession. 'I wasn't thinking straight, and somehow it all got out of control.'

She swallowed, remembering how helpless she had been to resist the soaring excitement, how hungrily she had kissed him back. It hadn't been all Jack's fault. The colour deepened in her cheeks. 'It doesn't matter,' she muttered.

'I didn't frighten you, Ellie, did I?' he said, shooting her a quick glance.

The only thing that had frightened her had been the power of her own response. 'No,' she said in a small voice.

'I was afraid I might have done. You looked...' Jack trailed off, remembering how dark and desperate her eyes had been. 'Upset...' he finished lamely.

'I was OK.' Ellie turned her face away to hide the colour burning in her cheeks. 'It caught me a bit off-balance, that was all.'

Off-balance. That was a nice, understated way to describe how she had felt as the world reeled around her.

Jack eased the joystick to the right, sending the plane into a gentle curve. 'Ellie, are you sure you want to go ahead with this?' he asked. 'I know I wasn't very understanding at the time, but that party made me realise how difficult it's going to be for you to be married to me and pretend that everything's fine when all you want is to be with someone else. I didn't make things any easier by carrying on like that, either. I wouldn't blame you if you'd changed your mind after the way I behaved.'

'Are you trying to tell me that you've changed *your* mind?'

'No.'

He had, of course, several times—and changed it back again as often. He felt uncomfortable whenever he thought about that party. His reaction to Ellie had disconcerted him. Clare and Gray hadn't noticed her with all those men, and it was obvious that they thought that he had been imagining it. But why would he do that unless he had been jealous, which he wasn't? He couldn't be jealous of *Ellie*.

No, he had been tired, edgy, confused, maybe, but definitely not jealous. Ellie was... Well, she was just Ellie. Or she had been until she'd put that dress on, he remembered darkly.

He cast a sideways glance at her averted face. When he had seen her waiting for him at the airstrip in her old jeans and a faded green shirt he had been relieved, but also more than a little embarrassed. It seemed hard to believe that he had got in such a state about Lizzy's little sister. Ellie was someone he looked out for, someone comfortingly familiar, not someone who drove him into a fury and then melted into his arms.

He hated the idea of her being hurt, of course, but that didn't mean anything. If he had a sister of his own, he would feel exactly the same.

'What I'm trying to say is that you don't have to do anything you don't want to do,' Jack went on after a slight pause. 'I know it might be awkward to cancel the wedding just after we've announced the engagement, but we could think of some excuse. We could pretend that we wanted to postpone it or something. People would soon forget.'

'I don't want to cancel the wedding,' said Ellie quickly, before he managed to talk himself out of the whole idea. 'I haven't changed my mind either.'

She drew a deep breath. 'I owe you an apology, too, Jack. It takes two to argue and two to kiss. When things got out of control at the party, it was my fault as much as yours. Perhaps we should just pretend it never happened?'

Jack shot her a grateful look. 'If you're happy to forget about it, Ellie, then so am I.'

Forget about the way he had kissed her? There was fat chance of that, thought Ellie.

'At least one good thing came out of that party,' she said, mustering a smile and hoping that she sounded suitably cool and composed, and not as if her heart was somersaulting around her chest at the mere thought of that kiss. 'It completely convinced Lizzy that we were a real couple.'

'Really?'

'I was surprised, too,' said Ellie. 'But Lizzy seemed to think that the fact that we were arguing was a very good sign—I'm not quite sure why. She even said that she envied us!'

Jack didn't feel as if there was anything about his situation for anyone to envy. 'She wouldn't say that if she knew the truth,' he said with the faintest shade of bitterness.

Ellie looked down at the land that rolled like an endless greenish-grey carpet out to the horizon and beyond, at the vast expanse of scrub where the cattle hid beneath the spindly gums and termite mounds rose like castles out of the red earth.

'No, I don't suppose she would,' she agreed dully.

There was a silence which for some reason felt awkward. It was Jack who broke it first.

'I thought Lizzy was a believer in waiting until you had found your soul mate and only getting married if everything was romantic and perfect.'

'She is.' Ellie kept her eyes on the bush below them. 'We obviously put on a better act than we realised.'

'We must have done.'

There was a strange note in Jack's voice and Ellie could feel him watching her. Her skin prickled beneath his eyes, and the colour rose in her cheeks as she imagined Jack wondering how she had been able to put on quite such a convincing performance of being in love with him.

'I asked Lizzy once if she had ever been in love with you,' she said, in a desperate attempt to steer the conversation away from her own eager response to his kiss.

At least she succeeded in diverting Jack. 'What did she say?' he asked, half-startled, half-amused.

'She said that she hadn't, but she didn't know why not. You're such good friends, and you've got so much in common. I always thought that you and Lizzy would end up together,' Ellie confessed, amazed at her own composure. She really sounded as if she hadn't really cared one way or another, as if it had been no more than a matter of vague curiosity.

'I've never thought about it before, but now you come to mention it, it *is* funny,' said Jack slowly. 'I guess I always knew that it was Gray she loved. I couldn't believe it when she broke off their engagement, although I can see now that she was right. I don't think it ever occurred to me that Lizzy and I would be anything other than good friends,' he went on after a moment. 'I don't know why. She's a very special person.

'Pretty, too,' he added, an affectionate smile touching the corners of his mouth. 'It's odd that I never fell in love with Lizzy, but I did with Pippa. Pippa wasn't blond, but she was like Lizzy in lots of ways.'

A shadow crossed Jack's face as he remembered Pippa. 'She was warm and funny and lively, just like Lizzy is, but I don't go weak at the knees when Lizzy touches me, and the sun doesn't come out when she smiles. Do you know that feeling, Ellie?'

Ellie thought about the way the earth seemed to shift beneath her feet whenever Jack so much as brushed a finger against her. She thought about how the world took on a dazzling clarity when he was near, how the stars would brighten and the air would crispen and all her senses would tingle just knowing he was there.

'Yes, I know that feeling,' she said. She looked at the horizon, faint and blue and blurry in the far distance. 'There's no accounting for why we fall in love with one person and not another.'

Jack glanced at her averted face and found his eyes resting on the pure line of her cheek, on the warm curve of her mouth and the way her hair curled softly behind her ear, and he felt an unaccountable tightening around his heart.

'No,' he agreed in a voice that sounded shorter than he'd intended.

There was another pause. He made an unnecessary adjustment to the plane's course and tried to concentrate on the instruments in front of him, but Ellie was tugging annoyingly at the edge of his vision. His eyes flickered sideways just as she risked a glance at him, and even though they both looked quickly away, Jack was left feeling a fool for some reason.

'What about your parents?' he asked a little too heartily. 'Did we manage to convince them as well?'

'I don't think it would ever occur to them that we might be pretending,' said Ellie frankly. 'They're not exactly suspicious types. Mum's already obsessed with wedding dresses and floral arrangements,' she went on, seizing the chance to move the conversation onto less dangerous ground. 'She's determined that it'll be a traditional wedding. We've already had a row because I won't get married in the church at Mathison.'

'What's wrong with the church?' asked Jack. 'I don't mind, if that's what you want.'

'Churches are for real weddings,' said Ellie a little wistfully.

'Isn't ours going to be a real wedding?'

She turned her clear gaze on him. 'You know it isn't, Jack. I think the wedding should be at Waverley Creek. Waverley's the reason we're getting married. You want to marry me so that you can live there with Alice, and I'm marrying you so that I can live there rather than in the city.'

'Very clearly put,' said Jack, a slight edge to his voice.

'I'm just being honest. Our marriage isn't going to be real in the way it would have been real if you'd married Pippa,' she said with a little difficulty, 'and we've agreed that the vows we make aren't going to be binding. It's Waverley that binds us together, isn't it? Don't you think it would be better if we had the wedding there?'

A muscle was beginning to twitch in Jack's jaw. 'If that's what you want,' he said curtly.

Ellie looked down at her hands. 'It's not a question of

what I want,' she said sadly. 'It's a question of what would be the most appropriate, given our situation.'

She stole a glance at Jack's profile, but there was something daunting about his complete lack of expression. 'I, er, thought we could clean up the old woolshed,' she went on hesitantly when Jack said nothing. 'It's a lovely building. It's still got a roof, and it would just need to be cleared out and swept. I think it would be a great place for a party.'

'Good idea,' Jack agreed, trying to summon up some enthusiasm.

The trouble was that he didn't feel very enthusiastic. He felt flat and oddly dissatisfied. It was something to do with the way Ellie kept reminding him of just why she was marrying him, with her bright, impersonal conversation as she chatted on about the plans she and her mother were making for the wedding.

Jack didn't want to talk about the wedding. He wanted to know whether the kiss had shaken her as much as him. He wanted to know what she had felt, if she had lain awake every night since then, reliving it and wondering just what had happened.

They finished painting the homestead that weekend. 'I'm borrowing a couple of men from Bushman's Creek next week,' Jack told Ellie as she rinsed her paintbrush under the tap. 'We'll fix up the stockmen's quarters first, then we can make a start on the cattleyards.'

'Great,' said Ellie, trying not to notice how polite and distant Jack always was now. 'What time do you want to pick me up?'

Jack didn't quite meet her eyes. 'It's OK,' he said, 'We can manage. Things have been a bit busy at Bushman's Creek lately, especially with me spending so much time

over here, but Gray's said he can spare Jed and Dave for
a month or so, until I can find some men to work here
for the new season.'

'I could help, too,' she offered. 'I don't mind what I
do.'

'I think you'd be better sorting out the wedding,' said
Jack. 'It's not that long now, and there's still a lot to
organise.'

'Mum and Lizzy seem to be happy to do all that.'

'Still…' He hesitated. 'There's no need for you to be
here just yet.'

What he meant was that he didn't want her there. Ellie
felt as if she had been slapped. Jack obviously thought
she was only good for women's work, for cleaning the
house, for making the home. He had no more use for her
until he needed her to look after Alice.

Refusing to let him see how hurt she was, she put up
her chin and flashed a brittle smile. 'Fine,' she said.
'There's no point in me being here if you don't need me,
is there?'

So Ellie was stuck at home, bored and restless, trying
to show an interest in bouquets and tablecloths, while her
mother and Lizzy fussed daily on the phone about who
was wearing what and what everyone would eat.

She was ordered to Perth, where Lizzy swept her off
to buy a wedding dress, but being in the city only made
her feel more lonely and out of place. Ellie stood obediently and let herself be bullied in and out of elaborate
confections, but all she wanted was to be back at
Waverley, where the station was coming to life without
her, and where she wasn't needed.

The thought of Waverley kept her going. She longed
for the wedding to be over. When the dress had been
worn and the flowers had died and the guests had gone,

she would be at Waverley, with Jack, and with Alice, and she would be needed. Everything would be all right then.

They were married a month later.

'I cannot *believe* my little sister is getting married before me!' Lizzy pretended to grumble as she walked around Ellie, inspecting her with a proprietorial air and twitching the folds of her dress into perfect place. 'I'm obviously doomed to be the only spinster left in Australia!'

'You'll find someone Lizzy, and he'll be perfect.'

'If I don't, it will be your fault for insisting on having me as your bridesmaid,' said Lizzy darkly. 'This is the third time I've had to do this. You know what they say—three times a bridesmaid, never a bride!'

'Well, you're not really a bridesmaid,' Ellie tried to placate her. 'I just want you there for moral support.'

'I know,' said Lizzy with a grin. 'I'm just joking. Wild horses wouldn't have stopped me holding your flowers for you today—as long as you make sure that I'm the one who catches the bouquet!'

Picking up a spray of native flowers from the chest, she handed them to Ellie. 'There!' She stood back to admire the effect, and her face softened. 'You look beautiful, Ellie.'

Ellie turned almost reluctantly to look at herself in the mirror. Lizzy had insisted on making her up, and now it was as if a stranger stood staring back at her, a stranger with luminous green eyes and a warm, sultry mouth. Her brown hair was drawn back with jewelled clips to reveal a delicate bone structure that Ellie had never even known that she possessed, but her face felt stiff and unfamiliar, and she grimaced just to see whether her reflection would grimace back and convince her that it really *was* her in the mirror.

'It's a lovely dress,' Lizzy went on encouragingly. She had picked it out and had practically had to force Ellie to try it on, so she had a proprietorial interest in it. 'That ivory colour is perfect for you.'

Ellie glanced down at the dress a little dubiously and fiddled with the fringe of a sheer stole that Lizzy had draped artistically over her arms. She could see that it was a beautiful dress, long and sleeveless and cut with a stunning simplicity, but it just didn't feel like *her*, any more than the lipstick and the mascara and the pretty clips in her hair felt as if they belonged on her.

'I wish I could have got married in my jeans,' she said with a tiny sigh, and Lizzy looked shocked.

'Jeans! Honestly, Ellie, what is the matter with you?' she demanded. 'You're walking out that door to marry the nicest, sexiest, best-looking man in the district, and you want to wear *jeans*! Don't you want Jack to look at you and be bowled over by how beautiful you are?'

For a treacherous moment, Ellie let herself imagine what it would be like if Jack saw her and fell head over heels in love with her, just as she had always hoped that he would one day.

'Of course I do,' she said wistfully, wishing that she could believe that it might happen.

This was the day she had dreamt about for as long as she could remember. In a few minutes she would walk out through the door and marry Jack, but it wasn't the golden, laughing Jack of her dreams, Jack with the warm, dancing brown eyes and the smile that clutched at her heart. She was marrying a Jack whose eyes were wary, whose smile was rare, a Jack she had hardly seen for almost three weeks.

He had met her at the Waverley airstrip when she had arrived with her parents and Lizzy earlier in the day, and although he had smiled, he had made no effort to speak to her alone. He had said simply that he would let them have the homestead to get ready in and would see them at five o'clock. He might have been arranging to meet for a beer for all the sense of occasion he'd shown.

'Well, then.' Lizzy gave the folds of her dress a final twitch. 'Are you ready to go?'

Ellie took a deep breath. 'I think so.'

'How do you feel?'

'Terrified.'

It was true. The realisation of what she was about to do hit Ellie without warning with the force of a steam-roller, sending the breath whooshing from her lungs in a rush of sheer panic. She was wearing a wedding dress. She was going to get *married*.

But Lizzy only laughed. 'You'll be fine,' she said, picking up her own flowers and opening the door with a flourish. 'Just keep thinking of Jack.'

It was just after five o'clock when Ellie took her father's arm and walked across to the old woolshed.

Built in Waverley's glory days, its stone walls and curved roof had stood up to the years of neglect far better than the other station buildings, and now it had been transformed. Where teams of shearers had once worked their way through thousands of sheep, temporary tables covered with pale pink cloths had been set up and decorated with creamy-coloured flowers flown in specially from Darwin, and trays of glasses gleamed in anticipation of the champagne that would be opened as soon as the ceremony was over.

When Ellie and her father appeared, the woolshed was full of wedding guests. They turned as if one, parting to let her walk through them on trembling legs to where Jack waited with Gray at his side.

For Ellie, it was all a blur. She had a confused impression of smiling faces, but they seemed to be separated from her by an invisible curtain. She felt curiously detached, as if in a dream, and she found herself clinging to tiny details to convince herself that this was actually happening and that she really was on her way to marry Jack. She could feel the wiry strength of her father's arm, the hard wooden floor beneath her feet, the dull swish of silk against her legs as she walked.

And then, suddenly, Jack was there, turning to watch her approach, tall and devastatingly attractive in his formal suit, his expression so sombre that Ellie's heart turned over. Her step faltered and she would have stopped if her father hadn't borne her on regardless.

We shouldn't be doing this, she thought in sudden panic. I shouldn't marry Jack when I know he doesn't love me. He shouldn't marry me when he's still in love with Pippa. It's all wrong.

It *was* all wrong, but it was too late to do anything about it. Everyone was there, people she had known her whole life, all watching expectantly. Lizzy was behind her, her mother was already sniffling into a handkerchief, her father was beaming. And now they had reached Jack's side and her father was stepping aside, leaving her alone and stranded with no one to turn to but Jack.

With a sense of fatality Ellie took the hand he held out to her, and lifted her eyes to look into his face at last.

Jack had been feeling slightly sick. Waiting with Gray for Ellie to arrive, he had run his finger around his unfamiliarly tight collar and wondered what on earth he was doing there, about to marry a girl he didn't love—a girl, more to the point, who didn't love him.

He had thrown Gray a glance of desperate appeal, hoping that his brother could come up with some way to help him out of this mess he had got himself into, but Gray had been smiling at Clare, who was standing a little further along, with Alice in her arms. Jack had followed his gaze, and at the sight of his daughter, his nerves had steadied.

Alice was the reason he was here.

Behind him, the crowd stirred in anticipation, and he turned to see Ellie coming towards him on her father's arm. At least, he assumed it was Ellie. She looked so cool and so poised, so elegant in the long white dress, that Jack was shaken by sudden doubt that it was Ellie at all. She had done something to her hair, too, and the pure lines of her face and throat stood out with startling clarity.

Jack stared, gripped by sudden panic. He couldn't marry this stranger, walking towards him with her eyes demurely lowered!

She had reached his side and he put out his hand, hardly aware of what he was doing. Her fingers trembled in his, but when she looked up her eyes were clear and true and troubled. Ellie's eyes.

Almost giddy with relief, Jack smiled down at her. This was no cool, beautiful bride. This was the Ellie he had always known. Ellie who was hating this as much as he was. This wasn't the wedding she had wanted either, he reminded himself. Holding her hand tightly, he turned towards the celebrant.

It wasn't a long service. Ellie stared blindly ahead of her. The celebrant spoke about marriage, but the words seemed to wash over her, and then she heard her own voice, as if it belonged to someone else, making the right responses. Jack must have done the same, for the next moment she was holding out her hand, and he was sliding the ring onto her finger. Ellie could feel the warmth of his touch, the smooth, cool gold against her skin, as the celebrant pronounced them man and wife.

Man and wife.

Dazed, Ellie stared down at the ring on her hand. They were married. She was Jack's wife.

Slowly, she lifted her head, to find Jack watching her with warm understanding in his eyes.

'You may kiss the bride.'

Jack's smile was crooked as he looked down into Ellie's face. He had to kiss her, he thought, although after the last time it was probably the last thing she wanted. He couldn't *not* kiss her, not when all her family and friends were watching expectantly with sentimental smiles, but he could make it as easy on her as possible.

Taking her face between his palms, he touched his mouth to hers. It was only for a moment, hardly long enough to be called a kiss at all, but as their lips met Jack felt something unlock inside him, and he had an insane urge to gather Ellie into his arms and carry on kissing her.

The impulse was so strong that Jack had to wrench his mouth away. Oddly shaken, and unable to meet her eyes, he took Ellie's hand instead, and forced a smile as they turned towards their guests.

Ellie saw Jack smile and guessed at the effort it cost him to pretend that this was the happiest day of his life. She had felt his instinctive recoil as he kissed her, and her heart ached for him. He had hardly been able to bear to kiss her, the bride he had never wanted. She longed to comfort him, tell him that he didn't have to go through with it after all, but even as the words trembled on her lips she knew that it was too late.

It was done. They were married. And there was no
time to do anything more than brace themselves for the
flurry of congratulations that soon swept them apart.

The reception was almost as much a blur as the ceremony for Ellie. People kept telling her that she looked
radiant, but she couldn't help thinking that they were just
saying it because that was what you said to a bride, regardless of how she looked.

She didn't feel radiant. She felt disconnected and
alone. Jack had Alice in his arms, and he held her close
with his big, strong hands. Overwhelmed by the crowd,
Alice clutched at her father, burying her face shyly in his
neck, and Jack's expression as he bent his head to murmur reassuringly to her told Ellie everything she needed
to know, if she hadn't known already, about why he had
married her. He and Alice were two parts of a whole.
They didn't need her to feel complete, not the way she
desperately needed them.

Ellie's heart twisted, and she looked away to find that
Clare was watching her with such understanding and
sympathy in her expression that Ellie's chin came up. She
didn't need anyone to feel sorry for her, and she wasn't
going to feel sorry for herself. It wasn't as if she hadn't
known exactly what marriage to Jack would involve. She
had made her choice, and she was going to make the best
of it.

She smiled at Clare, a bright, defiant smile, and she
kept on smiling. She smiled through the photographs and
the speeches, she smiled as she cut the cake. She even
smiled when guests who had only just discovered that
Alice was Jack's daughter commented on their closeness.
Ellie was sure that she could read pity in their eyes, as
well as a kind of satisfaction at having Jack's puzzling
decision to marry her explained. Of *course*; he needed a

mother for his baby daughter. Why else would he have chosen boring little Ellie Walker as his wife?

No one mentioned the matter outright, of course, but Ellie was sure that was what they were all thinking, and as the evening wore on her smile began to look strained. Not that anyone else seemed to notice. The party was well away and no one seemed to be watching her at all.

Finding herself alone, Ellie seized her opportunity. Drifting unobtrusively back into a shadow, where thousands of fleeces had once been stacked, she allowed the smile to fall from her face. Oblivious to her, the party spun noisily on, and the woolshed resounded with the sound of music and laughter and dancing feet.

Through the crowd, Ellie caught a glimpse of Clare and Gray. They were just standing, observing the dancers, not even touching but somehow a unit, perfectly balanced and complete. As she watched, Gray ran his hand down his wife's spine in a gesture that was at once discreet and yet so sensual that something inside Ellie twisted with an envy so intense it was painful.

She saw Gray murmur something in Clare's ear, saw the secret smile that curled Clare's lips as she put her arm around his waist and leant into him. There was something so intimate about the way they stood there that Ellie felt her face burn, as if she had been caught peeping into their bedroom, and she looked quickly away, only to find herself staring straight into Jack's eyes. Her heart seemed to stop.

He was on the other side of the woolshed, watching her with a grave expression, and as their eyes met and held the music faded and the dancers whirled into a silent blur, and the two of them were quite alone, staring at each other.

Without haste, as if unaware of the other people around

him, Jack made his way across the floor to where Ellie stood, a slender, dark-eyed figure, her ivory silk dress gleaming in the shadows.

Ellie was suddenly very tired. She knew that she ought to fix the smile back on her face, and carry on playing the happy, radiant bride, but she couldn't. She couldn't move or speak or even think. She could only stand there and wait for him.

Jack came to a halt just in front of her, shielding her from the other guests, and his smile was twisted as he looked down into her face. 'You've had enough,' he said gently, and he held out his hand. 'Shall we go?'

CHAPTER SEVEN

ELLIE didn't answer. She just nodded and took his hand, and they slipped out of the woolshed by a side door.

Outside, the night air was cool and starry. Ellie turned her face up to the dark sky and breathed in its deep, tranquil silence. 'Thank you,' she said quietly after a moment.

'I saw you watching Gray and Clare,' said Jack. 'I saw your face, when you thought no one could see you.' He hesitated, remembering the nakedness of her expression. 'I know what it cost you to keep smiling all day. No one could have guessed that it wasn't the wedding you wanted.'

'It wasn't the wedding you wanted, either,' she said in a low voice.

There was a pause. 'No,' he agreed.

He was still holding her hand, and Ellie was very aware of him, a dark, solid figure in the starlight. The whiteness of his shirt gleamed in the darkness, and as her eyes adjusted she was able to make out more details: his tie where he had loosened it, his collar open around his strong throat, the rugged line of his jaw.

Her gaze drifted on to rest on his mouth, and it was as if she could still feel its warmth and its firmness as he kissed her, as if his hands still cupped her face, and a tiny shiver snaked disturbingly down her spine.

Pulling her hand away, Ellie began walking briskly towards the homestead. 'Do...do you think anyone noticed us go?' she asked, hoping Jack wouldn't wonder why her voice was suddenly so high and squeaky.

He shook his head, his slow, rangy stride keeping up with her without difficulty. 'The party's well away in there,' he said. 'Nobody would think it odd even if they did see us leave,' he pointed out. 'We *are* married.'

'So we are,' said Ellie on a tiny gasp. 'I just can't quite believe it.'

'I know,' said Jack with feeling. 'I told Gray and Kevin we didn't want any fuss, so I hope we'll be spared the usual high jinks. With any luck, anyone who did see us go will just think we're desperate to get to bed.'

'I suppose they would.'

There was a bleakness to Ellie's voice that made Jack wish that he had chosen his words more carefully. Now the image of newly-weds longing to fall into bed together seemed to jangle tauntingly in the air between them.

Ellie had reached the bottom of the verandah steps, and on an impulse Jack put out a hand to stop her. 'You don't need to worry, Ellie,' he said abruptly.

She looked at him with a certain wariness. 'What about?'

'About sleeping together.' He hesitated. 'We'll have to share a room tonight. There are so many people staying in the homestead that it would look odd if we didn't. But it's only for one night.'

His smile gleamed a little crookedly through the darkness. 'I won't lay a finger on you,' he promised. 'And when everyone's gone tomorrow, I'll move into the room next to Alice.'

'I see.'

'I guess we should have talked about this before,' Jack persevered, a little daunted by Ellie's lack of response. 'I just assumed that you wouldn't want to sleep with me.'

There was the faintest question in his voice as he finished. What did he expect her to say? Ellie wondered with a small spurt of anger. Oh, no, Jack, I want you to make love to me all night, every night? I want to lie in bed beside you and to be able to run my hands over your body? I want you to kiss me until I can't breathe, and then I want you to kiss me some more?

She couldn't tell him the truth, but if she didn't say anything she might never get the chance again.

'Well, I...' She trailed off hopelessly, not sure how to continue, or even what she had been planning to say in the first place.

'I know it's difficult for you,' said Jack quickly, seeing that she was floundering. 'You're in love with another man. Of course you're not going to want to jump straight into bed with me. I just don't want you to think that I ever expected that you would,' he finished, wishing that he could have phrased it better.

'I never thought that.' Ellie picked up her skirt as she turned to climb the steps, away from Jack and his tantalising nearness, away from the temptation to cast pride to the winds and simply tell him the truth. The effort of appearing composed made her sound almost cold. 'I never thought that you would want to sleep with *me*.'

'Didn't you?'

The dryness in Jack's voice halted Ellie with her foot on the second step, and the air leaked out of her lungs as she turned slowly, almost fearfully, to look down at him. He stood at the bottom of the steps, rangy and apparently relaxed. His jacket was slung over his shoulder, and he wore a quizzical expression that confused and unnerved her.

'No, I...I mean... Well, we said we'd be friends...' she stammered.

Jack looked at her, poised uncertainly on the steps, her wedding dress gathered in one hand and falling in soft folds. The satiny shimmer of the silk was reflected on her skin, so that she seemed almost luminous in the starlight, her eyes dark pools in her pale face.

'Yes, that's what we said, isn't it?' he agreed, one corner of his mouth lifting in a lop-sided smile. 'And friends is what we'll be.'

Ellie eyed him uncertainly. Wasn't being friends what he wanted?

She hesitated, but before she had a chance to ask him what the strange note in his voice meant, Jack had climbed the steps past her and was holding open the screen door as if they had been discussing nothing more than the chance of rain or the price of feed.

'Lizzy wanted to know where we were sleeping,' Jack went on in the same brisk, impersonal way as he led the way down the corridor. 'She knows we haven't moved in properly, and I think she wanted to make sure the bedroom looked nice for you.'

He opened the door into the main bedroom and gestured Ellie inside. Desperate not to brush against him, or do anything that he might construe as an unwanted invitation, she practically edged around him and into the room.

It was one of the last rooms she and Jack had decorated. Ellie could remember painting the walls and wondering if it would ever be a room they would share. Well, now it looked as if it would be, even if only for a night.

The floor was wooden, the walls plain, and there were slatted shutters at the windows. In daylight, the effect was one of spare, uncluttered coolness, but Lizzy had done her best to create a romantic atmosphere. There were flowers on the chest of drawers, a lamp threw a soft yellow pool of light over the bed, and a lacy nightie was draped invitingly over the pillows.

They saw it at the same time. 'Oh,' said Ellie weakly.

'No one could accuse Lizzy of not making an effort for you,' Jack tried to joke, and she glanced at him.

'No,' she sighed.

There was an awkward silence while the nightdress lay on the bed and seemed to mock them and the loveless marriage they had embarked upon. Unable to bear the sight of it any longer, Ellie went over to the bed and picked it up with an unconsciously wistful expression. It was a lovely thing, she thought as she pulled it through her hands, no more than a wisp of silk and lace, and it must have cost Lizzy an absolute fortune. It was perfect for a bride.

For a real bride.

Ellie could feel pathetic tears prickling her eyes and she blinked them back fiercely as she folded the night-dress with jerky movements and almost shoved it out of sight in the top drawer of the chest. She cleared her throat. 'It's very nice,' she said with a fine assumption of unconcern, 'but not exactly the kind of thing one wears to sleep with a friend!'

'No,' Jack agreed. He turned abruptly on his heel. 'I'm going to check on Alice.'

Left on her own, Ellie wandered restlessly around the room. Her body was thumping with strain, and her brain buzzed with tiredness, but she knew she wouldn't be able to sleep. How could she, when Jack was going to be lying right beside her, warm, tantalising, close enough to touch?

What if she talked in her sleep? What if she rolled against him in the night? How would she be able to stop herself from clinging to him and begging him to make love to her?

How was she going to bear being just a friend?

She was just going to have to, Ellie decided, coming to an abrupt halt. It was only for one night. She was getting into a state about nothing, because nothing was what would happen. All she had to do was take off her dress, wash her face, find her own sexless T-shirt that she had brought to sleep in and climb into bed. And when Jack came back she would say goodnight, turn on her side and go to sleep.

It would be easy.

Having talked herself into being sensible, Ellie found herself baulked at the very first part of her programme when she couldn't undo the complicated fastening at the back of her dress. She wriggled and squirmed and contorted her arms over her shoulders, but she couldn't quite reach the top of the zip, and in the end she gave up and went along to the bathroom to try washing her face instead. Surely she would be able to manage *that*.

The door of Alice's room stood ajar. Jack was probably still in there, giving her a chance to get ready for bed in privacy. Ellie kept her eyes lowered and walked quickly past, her skirt swishing along the polished wooden floor.

She felt better when she had brushed her teeth and washed the make-up off her face, and she made her way back down the corridor to the bedroom with her head held high. She wasn't going to spoil everything by making a stupid fuss now.

A movement in Alice's room caught her eye as she passed the door. From this direction she could see how the light from the corridor angled into the room. It just reached the end of the cot, where Jack was standing, staring down at the framed photograph he held in his hands.

As Ellie hesitated, he looked up, and even in the dim light she could see that his expression was one of such unutterable sadness that her heart cracked for him. She didn't have to be able to see the picture to know that it was the photo of Pippa that always stood by Alice's cot.

They looked at each other in silence, while Alice slept peacefully. There was no need for words. There was nothing either of them could say. Ellie could only gaze helplessly, hopelessly back at Jack and long for some way to comfort him. When the only way she could think of was to leave him alone with his grief and his daughter, she turned and walked softly on.

Her own feelings were so trivial compared to Jack's. Ellie thought about the sombreness of his expression as he watched her walk across the woolshed towards him on her father's arm. The whole day must have been agony for him.

It should have been Pippa standing next to him, Pippa who held out her hand for the ring, Pippa smiling in the photographs and laughing as she tossed the bouquet. How had Jack been able to bear looking at his bride today? wondered Ellie. How had he managed to smile when he saw her standing there next to him with her quiet, ordinary face, instead of the vibrant, beautiful Pippa?

With a sigh, Ellie sat on the edge of the bed and smoothed the cover sadly with her hand. Poor Jack, poor Pippa. All that love, all that laughter, and now there was nothing.

'Are you planning to sleep in that dress?' Jack spoke from the doorway, obviously making an effort to keep his voice light.

'No.' Ellie got to her feet, willing to follow his lead

and pretend that everything was normal. 'I can't undo the zip, that's all.'

'Come here, and I'll have a go.'

Jack moved into the room and Ellie turned towards him, only to stop as if teetering on the brink of an abyss. She couldn't do it, she realised with a blinding sense of certainty. She couldn't pretend that everything was all right when Jack's heart was broken.

'Oh, Jack,' she said unsteadily, and her voice cracked. 'I'm so sorry…'

Jack stopped, too. He didn't say anything. He just opened his arms, and Ellie walked into them.

They held each other close, and it seemed to Ellie that she was taking comfort as much as giving it. 'It must have been so awful for you today,' she muttered after a while. Her arms were tight around his back, her face pressed into his shoulder, and she could smell his warm, clean, reassuringly masculine smell. He moved with an easy, even lazy grace, but he was like a rock she could cling to, his body firm and solid and inexpressibly reassuring.

'And for you.' Jack laid his cheek against Ellie's hair and tightened his arms around her in a warm hug. She needed comfort, too.

Pippa's photograph had caught his eye as he'd bent over the cot to check that Alice was sleeping soundly, and he had picked it up slowly. Pippa had smiled joyously up at him, and Jack had ached with a renewed sense of loss as he remembered her brightness and her beauty. Her laughter had seemed to echo in the darkness above their sleeping daughter.

He had thought about Pippa a lot that day as he prepared for his wedding. She was the mother of his child, the dazzling star who had lit up his life and then disappeared, leaving it in darkness, and on his wedding day, of all days, he owed it to her to remember the girl he should have shared it with.

'I'm getting married for Alice, Pippa,' he had murmured to her photograph, but as he'd lingered by the cot his memory of her had kept blurring, unbidden, into thoughts of Ellie. Of the unhappiness in her eyes as she'd walked through the woolshed to marry a man she didn't love. Of the naked longing in her face as she'd watched Gray and Clare. Of the way she had looked in the starlight, with her wedding dress gathered in her hand and her gaze dark and questioning.

Jack held her now, very conscious of her softness and her slenderness. She felt warm and pliant and disarmingly right in his arms. He could smell her perfume, light and elusive, and the silk of her dress was cool and smooth beneath his hand as he rubbed her back with a slow, gentle movement, soothing her distress as he would a frightened animal.

Gradually, the strain eased out of Ellie's body. She relaxed into him with a tiny sigh, and the only sharp edge to her was the jewelled clasp, which felt cold and hard against Jack's cheek as he laid it against her hair. Without thinking, he unclipped first one and then the other, and let her hair tumble softly around her face.

Ellie didn't protest, but she did pull back a little in surprise, and Jack found himself looking straight into her eyes. They looked at each other, both conscious that as the silence lengthened the companionable comfort was trickling out of the atmosphere and leaving in its place something new and infinitely more disturbing, something that jangled insistently in the air between them and seeped under their skins.

Very slowly, Jack opened his fingers and let the clasps

fall to the floor with a clatter that reverberated in the quietness, but Ellie didn't react. She stood mouse-still, her eyes never leaving Jack's, while a quivering began deep inside her.

Jack lifted his hands to tangle them in her hair. 'Ellie…' he said in a deep voice, 'Ellie, do you think that just for tonight we could be more than friends?'

Tongue-tied by his touch, tantalised by his nearness, Ellie looked dumbly into his face. Her heart was slamming against her ribs in slow, painful strokes. She knew what Jack wanted. He wanted to forget his grief, to stop thinking and remembering and to lose himself for a while where the past and the future faded into insignificance and only the moment mattered. She couldn't bring Pippa back, but she could do this for him.

Her arms had fallen from him when he'd pulled the clasps from her hair, and now she lifted her hands to spread them against his chest, finding her voice quite easily after all. 'Would it help, Jack?' she asked gently.

The corners of his mouth lifted in a slight smile. 'I think it would,' he said gravely, his warm fingers grazing her skin as they drifted tantalisingly along her jaw and down her throat.

'I'm not pretending it will make everything right,' he went on softly, 'but it might make it easier for us both to get through this night. What do you think?' he added, his voice so low that it seemed to shiver over Ellie's skin.

'I…think it would, too.' Ellie was dry-mouthed, her senses already drumming in response to his slightest touch.

His hand had curved around her throat, was sliding under her hair to caress the nape of her neck. 'I don't want to force you, Ellie. You can say no. You know that, don't you?'

'Yes, I know,' she whispered.

With an agonising lack of haste, Jack pulled her back into his body. His lips were at her temple, warm, tantalising, almost thoughtful as they drifted over her cheekbone, along her jaw, to rest on the very corner of her mouth.

'It's just for tonight,' he murmured again, and Ellie managed to nod.

'I know.'

'You need some comfort, too, don't you, Ellie?'

She could feel his breath against her lips, and she closed her eyes against the wrench of desire. 'Yes,' she said unevenly. 'Yes, I do.'

Jack's mouth brushed over hers. 'You don't want to say no, do you?'

'No,' said Ellie. 'I want you.'

Her voice was barely more than a whisper, but the words seemed to echo around them, bouncing off the walls and booming in the air. *I want you, I want you.* It was true, but Ellie hadn't meant to tell Jack that.

'Just for tonight,' she added quickly, before he could recoil, just so that he knew that she understood.

'Just for tonight,' said Jack, and then his lips possessed hers, and Ellie gasped with a mixture of relief and excitement and a strange, heady sense of having come home at last.

She wound her arms around his neck and gave herself up to the intoxicating pleasure of being kissed by Jack the way she had always dreamed of being kissed. She knew that it wasn't real, she knew that it wasn't for ever, but for tonight it was enough to be in his arms, to be able to kiss him back.

They had made a bargain to forget everything for this one night. Tomorrow, they could go back to pretending, but now...now there was no need to hold back, and no fear that Jack would guess the truth. This was comfort; this was allowed. Jack needed it and wanted it as much as she did.

Jack gathered her tightly against him, his hands insistent as they slithered over the silk, and Ellie melded into his hard body, beyond thinking about anything but the taste of him and the feel of him and the trembling need inside her which grew stronger and more urgent with every kiss, every caress.

'You wanted me to undo your dress, didn't you?' Jack murmured seductively against her throat, his mouth so warm and his lips so enticing that Ellie tipped back her head with a tiny gasp at the desire that clutched savagely at her in response.

'I did,' she said breathlessly, and shivered anew as she felt Jack smile against her skin.

'I'll have to see what I can do.'

His hands slid caressingly over her shoulders and met at the top of the zip, where he found the fiddly hook-and-eye fastening. It took him longer than he had thought to undo it, but then his fingers weren't quite steady, and Ellie wasn't making things any easier by kissing his throat and fumbling with the buttons of his shirt.

Jack's senses snarled with mingled anticipation and frustration. On the point of giving in and simply wrenching the fastening impatiently apart, he muttered in relief when he somehow managed to get the thing undone, and he felt Ellie quiver with responsive laughter.

Kissing his way down her neck to the alluring curve of her shoulder, Jack took the zip between his finger and thumb and eased it with a luxurious, provocative lack of haste all the way down to the base of her spine. The slow, swishing sound of the unfastening zip seemed to sizzle erotically in the lamp-lit hush. Once it had gone as far as it would go, he traced his way back up to the nape of her neck with warm, enticing fingers that stroked and circled and teased until Ellie felt as if she was afire and would shatter in the spinning, searing delight.

Murmuring something that was half-protest, half-pleading, she clutched at Jack, but he was intent on sliding the straps of her dress off her shoulders. Slowly, he drew the dress down, until it slithered over her hips and puddled onto the floor with a sigh of silk, and then he reached round her to unclip her bra and let it drop beside the dress.

'Ellie…' He caught his breath, unprepared for the way she looked. She stood before him, slender, wide-eyed, her body softly curved, her skin glowing in the lamplight.

Jack felt as if a powerful force had slammed into him, lifting him off his feet and leaving him reeling and helpless. 'Ellie…' he said again in an unsteady voice, then stopped, unable to go on, unable to find the words to tell her how she made him feel, unable to do anything but gaze at her in wonder.

His stunned disbelief was so obvious that Ellie was conscious of a surge of exultation at her own power. She stood quite still, smiling at him, until with hands that were not quite steady he reached for her, and she lost all sense of time. He secured her against him with a new urgency and the fire between them exploded into a blaze. Kissing frantically, they pulled at his clothes, shedding them as they went, until they were both naked and Jack could draw her down onto the bed.

His hands moved possessively over her, very strong and sure against her softness, and he explored her with wonder, dipping and curving, gliding lovingly over the satiny warmth of her skin, his lips following his hands in searing patterns of desire until she arched beneath him, gasping his name.

He was so firm, so exciting. Ellie ran her own hands over him with a kind of desperation. She couldn't touch him enough, couldn't press herself close enough against him. She rolled over him, glorying in his strong, supple body, in the taste and texture of his skin, in the ripple of muscles beneath her questing fingers.

Caught up in the whirl of sensation, Ellie gave herself up to the timeless beat of desire, where nothing mattered but the hardness of Jack's body, the sureness of his hands and the wicked pleasure of his lips as he discovered her secret places, opening her up, unlocking her until she soared free.

Ellie had never known such an intensity of feeling. It was exhilarating, entrancing, electrifying. It was terrifying. Sobbing Jack's name, she dug her fingers into his back, and he murmured reassuringly to her as they moved together in an irresistible rhythm that bore them up to heart-stopping heights before it sent them tumbling and breathless at last into a dazzling explosion of release.

It was a long, long time before they slept. Reluctant to waste the night they had, they lay entwined in the shadows, learning each other anew, and later they made love again, slowly, tenderly, drenched in enchantment. They didn't talk. Words might have broken the spell. So they just held each other, and at last Ellie fell asleep in the curve of Jack's arm, her cheek resting on his chest where she could feel the steady beat of his heart.

Sunlight striping through the shutters woke Ellie the next morning. She lay drowsily for a while, eyes closed, emerging reluctantly from sleep and dimly aware that she didn't want it to be morning. Morning meant that the long, sweet night was over.

Turning her back to the window, Ellie squeezed her eyes shut against the light, but it was no good. She was awake, and the enchantment had evaporated with the dark. 'Just for tonight,' Jack had said.

'Just for tonight,' she had promised.

And now the night was over.

Lying in the morning sunshine, Ellie ached with the memory of the sweetness they had shared. She would never forget it, and never regret it, but she had to accept that it would never happen again.

The door opened and Jack came in, carrying Alice. He was wearing jeans and a sweatshirt, and he held a mug in his free hand. He set it down by the bed as Ellie pulled herself up onto the pillows, taking the sheet with her.

'Oh, good, you're awake,' he said, as if he had never whispered endearments into her skin. 'I've brought you some tea.'

'Thank you.' Ellie felt ridiculously shy in the bright morning light, and she was glad when Jack swung Alice down onto the bed. She could smile and hold out her arms to the baby at least.

Crowing with delight, Alice clambered onto Ellie, who welcomed her with a tight hug. Jack turned abruptly away and went over to open the shutters. 'There's no sign of anyone else,' he said.

Ellie made a heroic effort to match his conversational tone. 'They're probably all sleeping it off.'

'It must have been quite a night.'

Ellie concentrated on Alice, holding her little hands wide apart so that she could stand, gurgling proudly at her achievement. 'It must have been,' she agreed in a voice quite without inflexion.

Jack had been standing by the shutters, running his finger along one of the slats, but at that he came back to sit on the edge of the bed. 'It was quite a night for us, too,' he said quietly, and the breath dried in Ellie's throat.

'Yes,' was all she managed to say.

Ignoring Alice, who had lurched from Ellie's hold to clutch at his shoulder, he took Ellie's hand. 'I don't know how to thank you,' he said.

His fingers were warm and strong around hers. Last night they had curved around her breasts. Ellie swallowed and looked away. 'You don't need to thank me, Jack.'

'I do. Last night...' He hesitated, trying to find the words to tell her what it had meant to him.

'I know,' she said quickly before he could remind her that she shouldn't take it seriously. 'Last night we comforted each other.'

She drew her hand out of his, and when Jack made no attempt to hold onto it she lifted her chin proudly. She wasn't going to beg for something he couldn't give. 'I'm grateful to you, too, Jack. It would have been a long, lonely night without you, but you needn't worry. I'm not going to make a big deal out of it. We both know exactly where we stand, don't we?'

'Yes,' said Jack, deflated by her composure.

He wished the situation seemed as straightforward to him as it apparently did to her. She had been so sweet and so warm, and he could still feel the silkiness of her skin, the wildfire that had burnt between them. He had told her that he wanted comfort, but somehow comfort had become delight, and delight had blurred into passion, and passion had spun in its turn into something else, something fiercer and more urgent, something awesome in its power.

'Yes, of course we do,' he said again more firmly, in case Ellie suspected that he *didn't* really know where he stood any more. He had started to try and tell her that when he took her hand, but she had withdrawn it so quickly that he had lost his nerve. It was obvious that last night had been a one-off as far as she was concerned. She would be appalled and embarrassed if he said something now, and the last thing Jack wanted to do was to make Ellie uncomfortable.

'It was just one night,' Ellie continued, determined to make sure that Jack understood that she wasn't going to embarrass him by misinterpreting what had happened.

She couldn't look at him, though, finding it easier to watch Alice, who was happily oblivious to the awkward atmosphere and was using her father as a support, her tiny fingers clinging onto his sweatshirt as she edged her way round him on unsteady legs.

'Yes,' said Jack again, too conscious of Ellie's bare shoulders and her nakedness beneath the sheet to pay much attention to his small daughter's triumphant if somewhat wobbly progress.

Ellie stared down at the shiny new wedding ring on her hand as she twisted it nervously around her finger. 'It's not that it wasn't…it wasn't…' Oh, God, how could she tell him how wonderful it had been without convincing him that she was panting for more? She drew a shaky breath. 'I mean, it was good for me,' she said with difficulty, cringing at the pedestrian inadequacy of the words, 'but I think we should leave it at that, as we agreed.'

Jack was conscious of a spurt of irritation. There was

no need for Ellie to go on about it. He had got the point that she had no intention of sleeping with him again the first time.

Opening his mouth to snap back at her, he was diverted by Alice, who was taking a wild lunge back towards Ellie. Unable quite to make it without a step, she staggered, wavered and then lost her nerve, sitting down abruptly on her bottom. The bedclothes made a soft landing, but her face was a picture of frustration and determination as she took the easy option and crawled the rest of the way over Ellie's legs.

Jack felt something in himself relax at the sight of her clambering so trustfully over Ellie. He had forgotten Alice last night. She needed Ellie to stay and be a mother to her, and Ellie wasn't going to do that if she felt that he was trying to renegotiate the agreement they had made.

Ellie was right. They should draw a line under last night and pretend that it had never happened. It was much better not to complicate matters.

'Of course,' he said after a moment, and he even managed a smile. 'Shall we go back to being friends, the way we were before?'

Ellie forced an answering smile without quite meeting his eyes. 'Yes, we'll be friends,' she agreed.

She would be his friend, and he would be hers, and it would be fine, she told herself. It just wouldn't be like it was before.

Jack got to his feet and scooped Alice up from the bed. 'Time for your breakfast, young lady,' he told her, his voice just a little too hearty.

He stood for a moment, Alice squealing and wriggling with excitement under his arm, and something in his silence made Ellie lift her head and look up at him. As their eyes met Jack made a small movement, as if he were about to say something, but whatever it was, he seemed to change his mind.

'Drink your tea,' was all he said, and then he had gone, leaving Ellie staring after him.

CHAPTER EIGHT

THEY both tried, but somehow being friends was much more difficult than it had been before.

Jack was very glad that there was so much work to do. Gray's men were needed back at Bushman's Creek, but he had hired three more men for the season at Waverley, and they spent all day outside on the station, mending fences, checking watering points and making sure that the yards were ready before they began mustering in the stock to see exactly what they had and what kind of condition the herd was in.

The first muster gathered in dozens of horses that had run wild over the years when Waverley had been neglected. Separated from the cattle, they were corralled, and then Jack, who loved horses, spent hours working with them, coaxing them to the stage where they could be ridden.

Sometimes Ellie took Alice down to the yards after her afternoon nap to watch him. It was a favourite excursion for both of them. Alice liked to look at the horses, and Ellie liked to see how gentle Jack was with them. He would stand in the middle of the enclosure, talking softly to them as they laid back their ears and shied nervously away, looking utterly at home in his jeans and his boots and his battered cattleman's hat.

Her eyes would rest longingly on him. He was her husband, but the only time she could look at him properly was when he was absorbed in his task. Her gaze drifted hungrily over his lean figure and up to his face. His hat shaded his eyes, but she knew exactly how they creased at the corners, how white his teeth would flash if he turned and caught sight of Alice balanced safely on the wooden rail before her.

Ellie watched him, and squirmed with the need to touch him again. The memory of the night they had spent together was a fire that smouldered away inside her. She tried to keep it banked down, but it was hopeless when all Jack had to do was lift his hand or turn his head and it would blaze into life again.

Ellie dealt with it the only way she knew how. She was cheerful and friendly, but she was very careful not to touch him or to appear eager for his company, and she made no attempt to stop him disappearing into the office every night as soon as the men had gone.

Hiding her loneliness and frustration behind a show of activity, Ellie made a point of keeping herself busy. She would have liked to help Jack and the men, but there was more than enough to do around the homestead, what with looking after Alice, providing three meals a day for four hungry men, and keeping up with the normal washing, cooking and cleaning.

Desperate to get out of the house, even if only as far as the garden, she planned to grow vegetables, and she spent long hours digging and preparing a plot. It was hot, heavy work, but somehow soothing, too. Ellie would rub her back at the end of a session and contemplate the neatly tilled earth with satisfaction and a new sense of calm.

She had known it wouldn't be easy, but at least she was here, at Waverley, with Jack. It was what she had wanted, wasn't it? Jack might not be ready to think of her as more than a friend, but if she just got on with doing what she had agreed to do, and didn't alarm him or embarrass him, he might get used to her presence. He might change his mind. Ellie told herself that she just had to be patient.

The day Alice took her first step, Ellie was as thrilled as if she had been her own daughter. Exclaiming at her cleverness, she caught her up with a kiss and was about to rush down to the yards to find Jack when she stopped and put Alice carefully back down on the floor.

'I think Daddy will want to see you take your first step himself, don't you?'

'Dada!' agreed Alice obligingly.

Ellie hoped that Alice might show off her new skill when Jack came in to bath her that evening, but she just carried on stubbornly cruising around the pieces of furniture that she could reach, dropping down to a crawl if there was too big a gap to cross on her two legs. Ellie could almost have sworn that Alice was deliberately holding back until Jack was in the proper mood to appreciate her achievement.

She didn't show him what she could do until two days later. Ellie was back in the vegetable plot, while Alice sat nearby in the shade, almost enveloped by an enormous floppy hat. Ellie had given her some water in a bowl with an old plastic cup, and she was absorbed in her own experiments, chirruping with interest and pleasure when she saw what happened when she poured water onto the red dust around her.

When Jack found them, Ellie was sitting back on her heels, watching Alice with a smile. Neither of them saw him at first, and as his eyes moved from his grubby daughter to where Ellie crouched, her face shaded by a straw hat, her hands as dirty as Alice's and a gentle smile curving her lips, his throat tightened.

'You both look like you're having a good time,' he said, his voice absurdly dry.

Ellie's heart missed a beat, the way it always did when she saw Jack, and she straightened instinctively as he moved towards her with that lazy grace that was so typical of him. Taking off her hat, she made a show of wiping the back of her hand across her forehead, just so that Jack realised that the colour in her cheeks meant that she was hot and not that she was suddenly, ridiculously, shy.

'Alice certainly is,' she said, hating the effort she had to make to keep her voice light and controlled. 'That water has kept her happy for ages.'

'It doesn't take much to amuse her, does it?' Jack hunkered down beside Alice and tickled her nose. 'It would be nice if all we needed was a bowl of water to make *us* happy.'

He glanced up at Ellie as he spoke. His tone was joking, but beneath his hat his expression was serious, and when their eyes met, the air seemed to evaporate between them, leaving Ellie's mouth dry and her heart hammering.

'It would,' she agreed a little breathlessly. 'But things are never that simple, are they, Jack?'

Jack thought of his own confused feelings, of how he lay awake torn between loyalty to Pippa's memory and wanting to do the best for Alice, between grief and regret and the unsettling way Ellie made him feel, just as she was doing now, as she stood there with her face smudged with dirt and a trowel in her hand.

'No,' he said deliberately, 'they're not.'

A peremptory tug on his jeans made him look down at Alice, who preferred to be the centre of attention and was not at all impressed by the way the two of them were staring at each other and ignoring her. Grunting with the effort, she used his leg as a support as she pulled herself upright and stood, clutching at her father with one hand and with a rather uncertain expression on her face, as if she was not quite sure what to do with herself now that she had got there.

Not sorry for the excuse to break eye contact and look away, Ellie put down her trowel. 'She's almost ready to walk,' she said as coolly as she could. 'Why don't we see if she'll go to you?'

Keeping her fingers crossed that Alice would take the opportunity to show off, she lifted her away from Jack and crouched behind her, steadying her at the waist. Jack knelt on one knee, just out of Alice's reach, and held out his hands.

'Come on, Alice,' he said. 'Come to Daddy.'

Alice hesitated. 'Dada,' she echoed a little doubtfully, but Jack's smile was encouraging and she could feel Ellie's hands supporting her, so she took a step, and then another, too intent on reaching her father to realise that Ellie had let her go. And then Jack's hands were there, sweeping her up triumphantly, his face ablaze with an expression that made Ellie's heart contract.

'Did you see that?' he demanded. 'She was walking!'

Alice beamed, and looked so pleased with herself that in spite of the ache around her heart Ellie couldn't help laughing.

'She's a very clever girl,' she said. 'And she knows it!'

Jack was thrilled with his daughter's achievement. 'Let's see if she'll do it again,' he said, the slight awkwardness between them dissolved in the excitement. He set Alice down, and this time she went into Ellie's waiting arms. Her gait was decidedly unsteady, and sheer momentum got her most of the way, but she was un-doubtedly walking.

'Look how good she is!' said Jack proudly. 'Her first steps, and she's got the hang of it already!'

Ellie smiled, intensely glad that she hadn't spoiled his pleasure by telling him about the steps Alice had taken earlier. 'There'll be no stopping her now!' she agreed.

Alice was very pleased with herself, and with all the attention that she was getting, and the almost impercep-tible tension in the atmosphere faded as Jack and Ellie laughed together at her self-important expression. Every-thing would have been all right if they hadn't made the mistake of looking at each other again instead of at Alice.

Ellie was very conscious of how close Jack was. She could see the dust on his skin, the faint prickle of golden stubble on his jaw, the way his smile creased his cheeks, and she was shaken by a gust of such desire that her smile faltered and she got abruptly to her feet.

'It's getting late,' she said, and her voice sounded high and thin even to her own ears. 'I should go and get Alice some tea.'

Jack rose to his feet more slowly, swinging Alice up with him. 'We'll come with you,' he said. 'It's been a big day.' He tickled her on the nose until she chuckled and tried to bat his finger away with her hand. 'When I came to look for you, you were baby and now you're a toddler!'

He smiled proudly at his daughter, and Alice clutched her arms around his neck and buried her face in his neck, which was the closest she could get to a hug. Watching them, Ellie felt her heart constrict with love for them both so sharp and intense that she could hardly breathe.

'Did you want anything special?' she managed to ask,

wrenching her eyes away and beginning to walk back to the homestead.

'Oh, yes,' said Jack, reminded. 'I'm planning to muster the top end next week. It's difficult country up there, and you can't do much from the air. There are so many little gullies and places for the stock to hide that the only way to get at it properly is on horseback, but it'd be a long job with just the three of us.

'I've just spoken to Gray on the phone, and he's going to come over and help, but that would still only make five. He suggested that he brings Clare with him. She could stay here and look after Alice and you could come with us.'

Jack hesitated slightly. 'It would be useful if you could give us a hand, but you don't have to come.'

Ellie's face lit up. 'I'd love to,' she said, too thrilled at the prospect of getting out onto the station to object to being thought of as an optional extra, someone handy but not essential.

It would have been even better if Jack hadn't needed his brother to point out that she might be some use outside the kitchen, but at least she would be out, getting to know Waverley and doing a job she loved.

If she could show Jack how useful she could be if only he would let her, he might include her more in the running of the property. They would be able to fill up the ghastly silences when they were alone with talk about the station, and gradually they would get back to the way they had been before.

Ellie's imagination ran on unchecked. They would be friends, partners, easy in each other's company, and then maybe, if she was very patient, Jack would get used to her being there. He might even come to need her.

Suddenly life seemed full of possibility, and there was

a new spring in her step as she turned to Jack with a
smile. 'I can't wait!' she told him.

Jack blinked a little at her smile. Her eyes were green
and shining, and her face was vivid, as if he had offered
her the moon instead of a chance to ride for hours in the
hot sun and sleep in a swag on the hard ground.

He felt an odd tightening in his throat as he looked at
her. There was a smudge of dirt on her forehead where
she had wiped her hand, and her fingernails were encrusted with mud. Her hat was battered, and her shirt
shabby, but when she smiled like that somehow you
didn't notice all those things.

She wasn't beautiful, thought Jack, his eyes dwelling
on the curve of her cheek before drifting down inside her
collar, to where a pulse beat in the shadowy hollow at
the base of her throat. The sight of it gave Jack a sudden,
shocking memory of how it had felt to press his lips
there, and he jerked his gaze away.

She *wasn't* beautiful, he insisted to himself. Not really.
Not at all. She was just Ellie.

It had taken him weeks to put the memory of their
wedding night behind him. He wanted to be friends with
Ellie, the way they had agreed, but it wasn't easy when
she kept intruding on his notice in ways he hadn't antic-
ipated. Before the wedding, he had imagined them sitting
companionably together in the evenings, talking about
the day and their plans for Waverley, but that had never
happened. Instead he had found himself noticing little
things about Ellie that he had never registered before: the
tenderness in her face as she straightened the teddy bears
in Alice's cot when she kissed her goodnight, the
straightness of her back, the way she pushed her hair
behind her ear.

Once, he had thought of Ellie as someone quiet and

restful to be with, but not any more. Now she made him distracted and uncomfortable and vaguely irritated.

It wasn't her fault. Jack knew that. *She* was fine. She was as cheerful and friendly as she had always been, but she never gave any indication that their wedding night had changed anything between them. That should have made Jack feel better, but it didn't. It made him feel worse.

It wasn't too bad during the day, when he could lose himself in sheer physical work, or when Alice and the presence of the men at meals kept the silence at bay, but at night...at night it was much harder. Harder not to remember the pearly translucence of her skin, the silken length of her thigh, and the feel of her lips teasing their way down his throat.

Jack would lie in bed and stare at the ceiling, willing himself to forget the exact curve of her body that his hand had learnt as it swept possessively from her breast, dipping down to her waist and smoothing over her hip. He was trying his best to treat her as he had always done, but he hadn't found it easy.

He hadn't found it easy at all.

As the weeks passed, though, Jack's sense of vague unease had faded and he'd begun to think that he was overreacting. Everything was going well. Alice was happy, Ellie seemed content, and the men certainly appreciated her cooking. Gray's suggestion that Ellie join the muster had come at a time when Jack had been wondering how to get their relationship back onto the old footing.

It had seemed the perfect solution, and everything would have been fine if Ellie hadn't smiled at him like that and knocked him off-balance again.

What was it about her that was so disturbing? Jack felt

as if he had to be constantly on guard, and then felt ridiculous for feeling like that about someone who had never pretended to be anything other than an old, familiar friend.

He was preoccupied as he bathed Alice that evening. She was overexcited by her new-found skill at walking, and it took him longer than usual to quieten her. He stood by the cot, his hand on her tummy, remembering her face as she had realised that she could walk, remembering the laughter in Ellie's eyes as she opened her arms and let Alice stagger into them.

Jack frowned. He hadn't meant to start thinking about Ellie.

His eye fell on Pippa's photograph, and he touched it sadly. He wished they could go back to the way they had been when she was alive and everything had seemed simple. He had known exactly what he wanted then. He had wanted Pippa, with her beauty and her passion and her fire.

Pippa had pushed him to extremes—of happiness, of fury, and of bitter regret when she had gone. But even when things were at their blackest, he had always known exactly what he felt. There had been none of the confusion and unsettling doubt that he felt now.

Jack didn't even know what he was confused *about*. He just knew that he felt ridiculously hesitant about joining Ellie in the kitchen.

Ellie was standing at the stove when he went in. She looked up from the gravy she was stirring. 'What's the matter?' she asked after a single glance at his face.

Jack had taken considerable effort to compose his features into an expression of cool unconcern, and was annoyed to discover that it had been a complete waste of time.

'Nothing,' he snapped.

Ellie didn't say anything. She just looked at him with those clear eyes and Jack felt the inexplicable irritation fizzle out of him as if from a punctured balloon.

He sat down at the table and looked at his hands. 'I was just thinking about Pippa,' he said in a different voice.

Ellie bent her head over the gravy once more. 'You miss her, don't you?'

Jack sighed. 'I miss what might have been,' he said heavily. 'I miss what it would have been like if she'd been able to hear Alice say her first word, or if she'd been here today to see her take her first step. She shouldn't have died,' he finished, as if the words were wrung out of him.

'No, she shouldn't,' said Ellie quietly. 'It wasn't fair.'

Jack's chair scraped over the floor as he pushed it back and got to his feet, unable to settle. 'I thought it would be easier away from Bushman's Creek,' he said, prowling around the kitchen. 'There are no memories of her at Waverley, but somehow that just makes it worse.

'Pippa would have loved it here,' he went on. 'She would have been so happy with me and with Alice, just the three of us. Sometimes I can imagine it so clearly that I think I can hear her laughter.' He glanced almost defensively at Ellie. 'Does that sound stupid?'

'No, Jack. It just means you loved her and that you're grieving for her.'

Jack gripped the back of a chair, so hard that the knuckles showed white under his skin. Ellie wasn't even sure that he'd heard her.

'I just feel…' He groped for the right words. He wanted to explain to Ellie how the echo of Pippa's laughter was fading, how her image was blurring, how he clung to her memory because he felt guilty at letting it go. Pippa had given him Alice and he owed it to her to keep her memory as sharp and clear as it had been the day she had left.

'I feel as if she should be here,' he tried again. 'At times like today, when Alice walked for the first time, I imagine what Pippa would have done, how she would have looked, how happy she would have been, and she seems so close that I can feel her. But when I look, she's not there. *You're* there…'

Jack trailed off, unable to explain how she made him feel, how the ground that had seemed so firm seemed to shift beneath his feet and everything that he had taken for granted was suddenly uncertain.

There was a tight band around Ellie's throat as she stirred the gravy blindly. How stupid she had been to hope that Jack's memories of Pippa would fade eventually. How unfair to think that it would get easier for him to see her in Pippa's place.

She had been so eager to join the muster, so convinced that it would mark the start of a change in their relationship, so certain that she would be able to replace Pippa in Jack's life eventually. How crass of her to think that he could forget someone like Pippa!

He had turned to her for comfort on their wedding night, but comfort was all he had needed. She had known that, but it hadn't stopped her feeling hurt that he had avoided her since then. Of course he had avoided her, when every time he looked at her he saw Pippa's ghost hovering by her side with everything that might have been.

'I'm sorry, Jack,' she said with difficulty, knowing that there was nothing she could do to help. 'I wish things could be different. I really do.'

The soft brown curls swung forward, hiding her face, but Jack could hear the sadness in her voice, and it reminded him that Ellie had her own unhappiness to bear. He had forgotten the shadowy figure of the man she loved and who didn't love her back.

Jack wished that he had remembered him sooner. All the time he had been worrying about the disturbing effect that Ellie had on him, she had been dreaming of someone else and wishing, like him, that things had worked out the way they were supposed to! Jack was just glad he hadn't told Ellie how aware of her he had been. That would have made things really awkward.

He had hoped that realising Ellie's mind was elsewhere would make him less conscious of her, but it didn't work like that. He just carried on noticing the way her hair curled or the unselfconscious grace with which she moved, and pretending that he didn't. And the more he pretended not to notice, the more distant and disagreeable he became.

Frustrated, faintly humiliated by his inability to behave naturally with Ellie any more, Jack told himself that Ellie's indifference to anyone except the man she loved didn't bother him in the least. He was still in love with Pippa…wasn't he?

Wasn't he?

The very fact that he needed to question it made Jack uncomfortable, and the more uncertain he felt, the more he talked about Pippa to Alice, deliberately reminding himself of her liveliness and her spirit and all the ways she had been different from Ellie, holding onto her memory like a talisman against his doubts.

Ellie listened to him reliving his memories and told herself that she should understand. Jack was still grieving, and he needed to talk about Pippa, but it didn't stop her hurting at the way he shut her out.

Once, taking a bottle of milk into Alice's room, she saw Jack showing Alice Pippa's photograph. 'That's Mummy,' he was saying as he shifted her on his knee.

Alice looked up at her father. 'Mum-um,' she repeated obligingly, and Jack smiled.

'That's right. Mummy. She was beautiful, wasn't she?' He kissed the top of Alice's head. 'Just like you're going to be one day.'

Very conscious of intruding on a private moment, Ellie put the milk down on the chest and left without a word. Shaking, she went to stand outside and stood hugging her arms around her to stop herself crying. It was wrong to feel so jealous. Alice was Pippa's daughter. She needed to grow up knowing all about her. Ashamed of her own resentment, but tired of being made to feel second best, Ellie grew cooler and quieter, and hung on to the prospect of the muster.

Much as she loved Alice, she hardly ever got further than the homestead creek, and she longed to be out under the vast outback sky where she felt most at home. Ellie counted the days until they left, and as soon as she swung up onto her horse, her doubts fell away and she felt steadier, more balanced, herself once more.

It took them two days' hard riding to reach the foot of the range. It was wild country up there, with looming rocks and hidden gorges, but Ellie loved it. She sat easily in her saddle, savouring the space and the eerie stillness of the air, and the light that beat down around her.

When they stopped at last, they built a fire and heated the stew that Ellie had brought. Jack made damper, and they put the billy on the embers to make tea. At night, they rolled themselves in swags and slept under the stars, and Ellie was perfectly happy.

She was in the saddle again at first light, winkling out the cattle that had strayed deep into the gorges, chivvying them back to join the main herd that was being driven, rumbling protestingly, onto the plain. By the time the homestead came back into sight the herd had quadrupled in size and was a huge mass of heaving, snorting, bellowing beasts, half hidden in the thick cloud of dust raised by their hooves as they blundered on towards the yards.

Ellie was stiff and saddle-sore when she slid off her horse at the end of the last, long day, but she felt happier than she had for weeks, and Alice's obvious delight at seeing her again was balm to her sore heart.

Jack might not have come near her once while they were away, but Alice needed her. Ellie held her small, warm body and kissed her baby-soft cheek, and thought that as long as she had Alice and she had Waverley, that would be enough.

Ellie might have enjoyed the muster, but Jack hadn't. He wished he hadn't asked her to come. He'd tried so hard to ignore her, but it had been impossible when every time he'd looked round she was there, eyes shining, absolutely at home on her horse, in her element against the harsh landscape.

Jack pulled the saddle off his horse with a sigh. He had sat as far away from Ellie as possible around the campfire, but that had been a mistake, too. From where he'd sat he hadn't been able to keep his eyes off her as she'd talked quietly with the men, or gazed pensively into the flames, or leant forward to lift the billy off the fire.

It would have been easier if he could have told himself that she was just decorative, or disruptive, but of course she hadn't been. She had slotted easily into the team. She knew instinctively what to do. She could outguess a rogue bull and outride any of them. She had been one of the most useful people there.

He should have thanked her for her help, instead of curtly dismissing her to the homestead as soon as they got in. Irritable with guilt, Jack slapped his horse on the rump and watched it canter off into the paddock, kicking its heels.

'Muster went well.'

He turned at the laconic voice to see Gray, leaning his arms against the fence. 'Yes,' he agreed unenthusiastically.

'What's the matter?'

'Nothing.'

Gray raised his brows, but didn't pursue it. He waited until Jack had closed the gate behind him and fell into step beside him as he carried the saddle back to the shed.

'Ellie's a good person to have around, isn't she?' he commented.

Jack grunted.

Gray cast him a sidelong glance under his hat. 'She's pretty, too.'

Jack made a noncommittal noise. He wished Gray would shut up. It was all right for him, with an adoring wife waiting for him back at the homestead. Gray didn't know what it was like to live with someone who was a friend, someone it was getting harder and harder to think about in a friendly way, someone who was in love with another man and who had made no secret of the fact that she had married him for Waverley.

'You know, Jack, you're lucky to have her,' Gray went on, and Jack swung round, goaded beyond endurance.

'What do you know about it?' he snapped.

'Only what I can see with my own eyes.'

'Well, you can't see everything, all right!' said Jack savagely, and strode off with a thunderous expression.

His bad temper lasted well into the next week, long after Gray and Clare had returned to Bushman's Creek, and Ellie's hopes that the muster would mark a change in their relationship soon faded. Jack gave no sign of being prepared to involve her in the running of Waverley. He hardly spoke to her, except to tell her what time she could expect the men in for meals.

Hurt and bewildered by his attitude, Ellie would have welcomed even a return to the careful friendliness that had felt so uncomfortable before. Anything would be better than being treated as a mere housekeeper.

The sense of rightness she had felt after the muster had quickly evaporated. *Was* she doing the right thing? Ellie wondered. Yes, she was at Waverley, instead of stuck in some city office. Yes, Alice was adorable. But it *wasn't* enough, she realised at last, no matter how much she tried to convince herself that it was.

She didn't want to be a housekeeper. She wanted Jack to treat her like a partner.

Like a woman.

Like a wife.

CHAPTER NINE

BUT the more Ellie wanted it, the less likely it seemed that Jack ever would. She was appalled to find herself growing increasingly resentful of him, and threw herself into the household chores as if all the sweeping and scouring would somehow ease the loneliness and disappointment inside her.

She was scrubbing the floor in the living area one day when Jack came to find her. It was the first time that he had sought her out deliberately since the muster, and she was furious to discover that in spite of everything, her pulse rate still quickened at the sound of his voice.

'What are you doing?' Jack frowned irritably as he saw Ellie on her hands and knees. The corners of his mouth were turned down and he looked cross and ill at ease.

'What does it look like?'

After one quick glance, Ellie bent back to her scrubbing and sighed inwardly. What was it about Jack? He ignored her, he hurt her, he was grumpy and ungrateful, and still she loved him.

Everything would be so much easier if she could just stop loving him, she thought ruefully. If she could stop caring that he was obviously as unhappy as she was, stop hoping that he would come to love her in the end.

'There must be more important things to do than wash the floor in here!'

'Yes, there are, Jack,' Ellie agreed tightly, 'but not that I can do inside, right now.' She might be hopelessly in love with him, but it didn't stop her being exasperated

149

by the way he left her with all the household chores and then had the nerve to criticise the way she organised her time!

'Alice is asleep,' she went on between clenched teeth, 'and I need to stay somewhere I can hear her if she wakes. If I have to be stuck in the homestead, I might as well get on with some of the jobs I can't do when she's awake.'

The edge in her voice was lost on Jack. He grunted something that might have been an acknowledgement, and propped himself on the edge of one of the chairs, digging his hands into the pockets of his jeans. He was frowning down at his boots, lost in thought, and had clearly lost all interest in what she was doing anyway.

Typical, thought Ellie sourly, and vented her feelings on the floor, sloshing water out of the bucket and scrubbing with ferocious energy.

The sound of the brush grated in the silence, and Jack looked up with a frown. 'Can you stop that a minute?' he said irritably. 'There's something I need to talk to you about.'

Ellie sat back on her heels and looked at him warily. 'What is it?'

'You're not going to like it,' he warned her.

Apprehension clawed at Ellie's stomach. This was it, she thought in panic. He was going to tell her that he couldn't stand living with her any longer and wanted to end the marriage. He wanted her to go, and leave him and Alice and Waverley behind.

She swallowed. 'Tell me.'

She saw Jack hesitate, and braced herself for the worst, her fingers tightening around the scrubbing brush.

'I've just been talking to Scott Wilson.'

The relief was so great that Ellie dropped the brush. It

clattered unheeded to the floor while she stared at Jack, torn between a hysterical desire to laugh at the contrast between what she had been dreading and the innocuousness of Jack's remark, and the bizarre conviction that she had completely misheard what he had said.

'Scott?' she echoed cautiously.

'You know him, don't you?'

She wiped her hands on her jeans to give herself time to adjust to a conversation which was turning out to be very different from the one she had been expecting. 'Of course I know him,' she said carefully, still not quite convinced that she hadn't missed something important. 'He was at the wedding.'

'So he was.' Jack gave her a sharp glance. 'He was at the engagement party, too, wasn't he?'

'Yes. Why? Nothing's happened to him, has it?'

'He's coming to stay.'

'To stay? Here?' Jack nodded and Ellie blinked at him as she struggled to make sense of a conversation that seemed to be getting stranger and stranger. 'When?'

'Tonight.'

'*Tonight!* Why?'

'We're mustering those paddocks in the west tomorrow. It's ideal country to use helicopters and Scott's built up quite a business contracting for work like that. With him in the air, and the three of us on the ground, it shouldn't take too long. Scott said he'd fly up tonight and then we can start first thing tomorrow. I thought I should let you know that there'd be one extra to feed tonight.'

All this, just to tell her that she needed to peel a couple of extra potatoes! The exquisite relief Ellie had felt when she realised that Jack wasn't trying to find a way to tell her that their marriage was over was rapidly dissolving, leaving her with the dull realisation that absolutely nothing had changed. She hadn't even known that he was planning to muster those paddocks. She could have helped him there, too, but, no! All she was good for was providing meals!

'Fine,' she said in a flat voice.

'The thing is, Scott's coming up as a favour,' Jack went on. 'He's got several men working for him now, but they're all busy, so he said he'd come himself. He said I could consider it as a wedding present,' he added thinly. 'In the circumstances, I think we should offer him a bed in the homestead.'

Ellie eyed him in some puzzlement, wondering what he was leading up to. 'OK.'

Jack got restlessly to his feet. Clearly there was more to come. He went over to the window and stood looking out, his shoulders stiff with tension. 'You know what Scott's like,' he said. 'I've never known anyone talk the way he does. He keeps the local grapevine going single-handed.'

'So what?'

'So if he gets any inkling of the fact that we're not living as normal newly-weds, it'll be round the district in no time,' said Jack impatiently.

Ellie climbed stiffly to her feet, brushing down her jeans. 'I see,' she said slowly.

'You don't seem very bothered,' he accused her as he turned round. 'I thought you'd be concerned about your family hearing that things aren't quite as perfect as we've gone to so much effort to convince them they are.'

She met his eyes steadily. 'I am concerned,' she told him. 'What do you suggest we do about it?'

Jack dropped his gaze first. 'I think we should try and pretend that we're just like any other married couple,' he said. 'It will mean putting on a show, but we did it before and convinced everyone, so there's no reason why we shouldn't do it again.'

'You mean we should pretend that we're in love?'

The brown eyes flickered. 'Yes. Do you think you could do that?'

'I expect I could manage.'

Jack took a breath. 'I think we should sleep together tonight, too.'

Vivid colour surged into Ellie's cheeks and the air was suddenly charged with electricity. 'You know what I mean,' he said testily, swatting mentally at the memories crowding around him, memories of the silkiness of her skin, the taste of her lips, of the tantalising drift of her hands. 'I'm talking about sharing a room, that's all.'

'Scott may like to chat, but he's not the kind of person who goes around prying into bedrooms,' objected Ellie, equally unnerved by the memories jangling in the air between them. It seemed imperative to convince Jack that she was no more eager for them to sleep together than he was.

Jack shrugged. 'It's up to you. You're the one who wants to convince your family this is a proper marriage.'

It was true. If her parents got so much as a whiff of the fact that she wasn't as happy as she claimed to be, they would be there, demanding to know what was wrong, and Lizzy would be on the phone from Perth. The last thing Ellie wanted was to upset any of them. She had made her choice, and she would have to live with it.

'All right,' she nodded after a moment. 'That's what we'll do.'

When Jack had gone, Ellie finished scrubbing the floor, but her arm moved mechanically while her mind was on the night ahead. A slow shiver of anticipation tiptoed down her spine at the thought of lying in the dark next to Jack. What better chance would she have to rediscover the closeness they had once had?

Ellie didn't know what she could do to improve things, but she knew that she had to do something. The current situation was miserable for both of them. Being friends hadn't worked, so perhaps it was time to take her courage in her hands and ask Jack if he would consider being lovers instead.

He might say no. He probably *would* say no, thought Ellie, remembering his grim expression and the guarded way he held himself when he was near her, but it was worth a try. It wasn't as if she would be asking him to forget Pippa, just to recognise that she was a woman, too, and not just someone who peeled potatoes and scrubbed floors and changed Alice's nappy when he wasn't around.

Was that so much to ask?

It was the way she looked right now, Ellie decided as she washed her hands afterwards. In the mirror above the basin, her reflection stared despondently back at her, red-faced, grimy, hair lank and sweaty with effort. She looked awful.

No wonder Jack had sounded so unenthusiastic about the prospect of pretending to be in love with her again! Ellie grimaced at the mirror. What was the point of complaining that Jack only ever thought of her as a housekeeper when she never made the slightest effort to look like anything else?

Perhaps it was time she did.

Alice was asleep. The meal was ready. *She* was ready. All Ellie had to do was walk through the door and join Jack and Scott on the verandah. Instead, she dithered around in her room, trying to pluck up the courage to face Jack, terrified that he would know immediately what she was trying to do, terrified that he wouldn't even notice.

All she had done was change into a simple, soft swirl skirt in a pretty shade of blue, with a plain white sleeveless top. Her hair was washed so that it fell in soft, shining waves around her face, and she had put on one of the many lipsticks Lizzy had forced upon her over the years and which she normally never wore. It was hardly a show-stopping outfit, but Ellie felt ridiculously self-conscious as she hovered behind the screen door.

Taking a deep breath, she pushed it open before she had a chance to change her mind and went out. Scott and Jack were sitting in the old chairs drinking beers, but at the sound of the screen door they both looked round and got to their feet.

'Ellie!' Scott greeted her with a big hug. 'You look fantastic!'

Ellie smiled nervously as she hugged him back. 'Thank you,' she said, but her heart sank when she risked a glance at Jack. He was looking grimly unappreciative, his brows drawn together and his mouth compressed into a thin line.

'It's great to see you again,' Scott was saying, holding her at arm's length so that he could admire her. 'I didn't get a chance to talk to you properly at the wedding. When was the last time we had real chat?'

Very aware of Jack's set face, Ellie forced herself to concentrate. 'It must have been a few years ago. Before I went to the States, anyway.'

'That's right! Remember, I took you to the Bachelors and Spinsters ball just before you left?' Scott grinned. 'That was a great night, wasn't it? It's hard to believe

how much everything's changed since then. You heard
that I was married?'

'Yes, Mum wrote and told me,' said Ellie, turning a
little so that Jack wasn't looming at the edge of her vision. 'I didn't realise that you and Anna were that close.'

'We weren't. We never even liked each other that
much, and then one day...bang!' Scott snapped his fingers and laughed. 'It was like a bolt from the blue! I
can't believe I never realised before how fantastic Anna
was,' he confided. 'And when I found out that she loved
me back... Well, I guess I don't need to tell you two
what that's like!'

'No,' said Jack, but there was so much irony in his
voice that Ellie hurried into speech.

'I'm so glad you're happy, Scott.'

'Oh, I am. I never knew a man could be this happy!
You know all that romantic stuff about finding the other
half of you? Well, that's how I feel,' said Scott, beaming.
'You know what I mean, don't you, Ellie?'

Ellie's smile wavered. 'Yes, I know,' she said quietly.

Watching her, Jack saw her eyes darken with anguish,
and everything suddenly fell into place.

Ever since Ellie had been startled into dropping the
scrubbing brush at the sound of Scott's name he had had
his suspicions. Scott seemed an unlikely person for Ellie
to fall in love with, but it *could* be him.

The more he thought about it, the more convinced Jack
became that he had stumbled upon Ellie's secret. The few
clues she had dropped all pointed in the right direction.
She was obviously much closer to Scott than he had realised, and Scott's marriage to Anna could well have been
the reason she had decided that her feelings for him were
hopeless. Scott was based in Mathison, where Ellie had
wanted to stay so that she could be near him. *I just*

thought it would be easier being in the same place.
Wasn't that what she had said?

And Scott had been at the engagement party. Jack remembered how he had asked Ellie if the man she loved was there, and her face as she had nodded. 'Yes,' she had said.

It must have been a shock for her to hear that Scott was coming to Waverley, he realised. No wonder she had seemed upset when he'd told her! If he had known, he would never have asked Scott to help, helicopter or no helicopter. Seeing him, being with him, pretending to be happy, must be agony for Ellie.

It wasn't his fault, though, Jack's thoughts ran on, obscure guilt shading into disgruntlement. He wasn't telepathic. If Ellie didn't want to see Scott, all she had had to do was tell him.

Except that she clearly *did* want to see him. Jack's face darkened as he looked at Ellie and saw what an effort she had made to dress up for Scott. The sight of her when she walked through the screen door had been like a blow to his stomach. She never wore revealing tops or lipstick that drew attention to the warm curve of her mouth for *him*!

Jack wanted to stalk across the verandah and punch the cheery, complacent smile off Scott's face before dragging Ellie along to her room and forcing her to change back into jeans and a shapeless shirt that would cover her bare shoulders and hide her from Scott's appreciative eyes.

Instead, he turned abruptly on his heel. 'I'll get you a beer,' he said to Ellie.

Ellie watched him go in despair. It was all her fault. She couldn't carry off a feminine look, she thought miserably as she sank into a chair and summoned a smile for Scott. She should have just stuck to her old jeans. It must be blatantly obvious that she was doing her damnedest to seduce Jack, and not succeeding. No wonder he was looking so disgusted!

At least Scott thought she looked nice, Ellie tried to console herself. *He* didn't seem to think that she looked ridiculous. His cheerful friendliness and obvious pleasure at seeing her again were balm to her wounded feelings, and she turned gratefully towards him. Somebody had to make the effort to make him feel welcome, anyway, and it obviously wasn't going to be Jack. Without that baleful stare on her Ellie could relax and enjoy herself, talking to Scott about times when everything had been so much simpler.

In the kitchen, Jack heard her laugh and slammed the fridge door shut. They seemed to be quite happy out there without him! *Scott Wilson*, he thought in disgust, wrenching the top off the beer bottle. What in God's name did Ellie see in him?

It wasn't that he cared *who* she loved, but after all she had had to say about how much she loved him Jack had expected it to be someone a bit more special than Scott Wilson! Scott was the kind of bloke who talked too much and laughed too loudly at his own jokes, Jack thought disparagingly. Ellie would never be happy with someone like that. She needed someone to cherish her, someone like... Well, someone *not* like Scott, he finished to himself, unable to think of anyone worthy of her.

Not that Ellie seemed to think so. When Jack got back to the verandah she was looking relaxed and happy, with her legs curled up beneath her and her body turned invitingly towards Scott. Grimly, Jack set the beer down on the table next to her.

She glanced up at him and he noticed bitterly how she tensed at his nearness. 'Thank you,' she said.

Something about the way she flinched away as he pulled up a chair beside her caught Jack on the raw. He was supposed to be her husband, for God's sake! Very deliberately, he reached out and slid his hand beneath her hair. The nape of her neck was warm, the skin tender, her hair soft and silky against the back of his hand, and his fingers circled slowly in an instinctively possessive gesture. No harm in letting Scott know who she belonged to now.

'I'd do anything for you, darling,' he said provocatively, baring his teeth in a smile.

Scott gave a shout of laughter. 'I see you've got Jack just where you want him, Ellie.'

Burningly aware of Jack's lazily circling fingers, Ellie sat rigid and trembling, fighting the terrible urge to simply close her eyes and lean back into his touch. 'I wouldn't say that,' she said unsteadily.

'Wouldn't you?'

Jack's hand drifted down from her nape to the edge of her top, almost absently tracing its outline, from the narrow strap at her shoulder, down the scoop of the neckline and up to the other shoulder, and Ellie was unable to prevent a shiver as desire shuddered down her back and clenched at the base of her spine with such intensity that she had to bite back a gasp.

'No,' she managed with difficulty, and Jack jerked his hand away, consumed by a sudden fury—with Scott for his stupid comments, with himself for the way he was behaving, but most of all with Ellie for the way she flinched with distaste whenever he touched her.

'I see,' he said.

'Jack knows who's really boss,' chuckled Scott. 'Marriage is a wonderful thing, eh, Jack?'

'Wonderful.'

'You're a very lucky man to have Ellie.'

Jack wanted to hit him. 'I know,' he said, only just managing to unclench his teeth. He didn't feel lucky. He felt raw and confused and inexplicably depressed.

Ellie shot him a warning look. It had sounded as if the words were forced out of him. Hardly the way to go about convincing Scott that they were happily married! It had been Jack's idea to invite Scott, she thought crossly. He could at least make *some* effort. Scott was no fool. She could see his bright eyes flicking assessingly between the two of them. He was bound to guess that something was wrong.

'I hope you've bought a new car since I last saw you, Scott,' she said quickly, in an effort to change the subject.

At least she'd managed to divert Scott. 'The first thing Anna did when we got married was to make me get rid of it!' he told her ruefully. 'She said either the car went or she did.' He laughed. 'Remember that time we broke down on our way to the races?'

With that, they were off. Jack drank his beer morosely, forced to sit and listen as they reminisced. He hadn't realised that Ellie and Scott had known each other that well. For the first time, Jack felt his age. They were both eight years younger than he was, and they seemed to have spent a lot of time together. He listened glumly as they talked about parties and races and rodeos they had been to. He must have been at most of them, too, but they had clearly been too busy having a good time to notice *him* there.

It was a new experience for Jack to think about Ellie having friends of her own, a life of her own that had nothing to do with him, and he didn't like it. He took a savage pull of his beer. He was used to considering Ellie as part of *his* life, not of anyone else's and especially not of Scott Wilson's!

By the time Scott finally decided to go to bed, Jack could hardly bring himself to say goodnight. He was fed up with hearing about the parties the two of them had been to, parties where they might have kissed, where Ellie might have fallen in love. He was fed up with watching the way Ellie smiled at Scott, the way she laughed with him, the way she'd leant her elbow on the table and propped her chin in her hand, careless of what the other men would think of her flirting. She certainly didn't care what *he* thought, Jack decided sourly. She had hardly glanced at him all evening.

He had hoped that when the stockmen went back to their quarters Scott would take the hint and retire as well, but, no! Ellie had offered him another cup of coffee, another glass of wine, and Jack had had to sit for another hour listening to their interminable reminiscences.

At last Scott had let slip a yawn, and Jack had leapt to his feet. 'You must be tired, and we've got an early start in the morning,' he'd said, practically hustling Scott out of his chair. 'I'll show you to your room.'

He waited until he had seen the bedroom door shut firmly behind Scott before he went back to the kitchen, where Ellie was washing dishes with a kind of controlled fury. 'Sorry to break up your cosy little tête-à-tête,' he said nastily, 'but I want Scott working in the morning, and if it was up to you he'd never have got any sleep.'

Ellie crashed a saucepan onto the draining board. 'What cosy tête-à-tête?' she demanded. 'It's hard to imagine anything *less* cosy than the evening we've just spent, with you sitting there with a face like concrete! Why were you so rude to Scott?'

'I wasn't rude.'

'You hardly said a word all evening! You just sat there glowering and making everyone else uncomfortable.'

'I didn't notice you looking uncomfortable,' said Jack, scowling. 'You seemed to be having a great time!'

Ellie drew in a sharp breath. A *great time*? One of the worst evenings of her life, and Jack thought she had been having a great time? She controlled herself with an effort. 'Well, let's hope Scott thought so,' she said sweetly.

'I don't think there's any doubt about that!'

'In case you've forgotten, Jack, you were the one who said that Scott was doing us a favour, and as you made absolutely no effort to be pleasant I thought it was up to me.'

'Being pleasant?' he jeered. 'Is that what you call making a fool of yourself by tarting yourself up and flapping those eyelashes of yours at him? God, I don't think I've ever seen anything so pathetic! *Oh, Scott, remember when we went swimming?*' he mimicked cruelly in a falsetto voice. *'Oh, Scott, remember what a cute little girl I used to be?'*

Jack snorted. 'Do you have any idea how boring you both were? Remember this, remember that... Couldn't you have found anything more interesting to talk about?

'Like what?' Ellie was so angry at the injustice of it that she could hardly speak. 'Believe me, Jack, I would have *loved* to have had something else to talk to Scott about! But I don't suppose he would have been very interested in hearing me talking about cooking or washing or tidying up after you and Alice, and since that's all I've done since I married you. It was reminiscences or nothing. I dare say my past *is* pretty boring to you, but I can assure you that it's a lot more entertaining than my present. Do you have any idea how boring *that* is?'

Jack's mouth tightened. 'What's wrong with it?'

'I do nothing but cook for you, clean for you and look after your daughter for you, Jack, and I get no thanks for it. I'm stuck in the homestead all day. I never get to go anywhere or see anyone or do anything.'

'It never bothered you before,' he pointed out.

'Well, it bothers me now,' she said flatly.

'You knew what was involved,' he accused her. 'If you don't like being a housekeeper, you shouldn't have offered to be one.'

Ellie went white. 'I offered to be your wife, Jack, not your housekeeper,' she said in a frozen voice.

'It's the same thing.' Jack prowled irritably around the kitchen. 'We had an agreement. You wanted to stay in the outback and I wanted someone to help me look after Alice. That's what happened.'

'We agreed that we would be partners!'

'You own half of Waverley, Ellie,' he reminded her coldly. 'How much more of a partner do you want to be?'

Ellie pulled out the plug and watched the soapy water drain away like all of her hopes. What was the point of arguing? Jack just didn't understand. 'I want to be involved,' she said hopelessly. 'You never tell me what you're doing.'

'I can't come running back to the homestead every time I decide to do anything,' said Jack impatiently. 'There's no point in whining now, Ellie. That's just the way things are. You knew how it would be when we got married, didn't you? *Didn't you?*' he repeated savagely when she only shook her head.

'Yes,' said Ellie in a voice devoid of all emotion. 'You're right. I did.'

For some reason, her agreement only made him even more angry. The trouble she had taken to make herself look beautiful for Scott, the warmth of her smile, the way she had leant towards him, all had left Jack raging and confused, and now he lashed out, not knowing why, knowing only that he wanted to hurt her.

'In that case I suggest you get on with what you agreed to do,' he said bitingly, 'instead of whingeing that you're not involved, exchanging your dull stories with your dull friends, and dreaming about your pathetic little love affair that never even happened!'

Ellie stared down at the tea towel she was using to wipe her hands. It had a pattern of blue-and-red checks, faded through frequent washing, and there was a stain in one corner. She felt cold and very sick.

So that was what Jack thought of her. *Dull. Whingeing. Pathetic.*

Was that how she was?

There was a black mist swirling around her. Very carefully, Ellie hung the tea towel on the back of a chair and turned blindly for the door.

'Where are you going?' Jack demanded furiously.

'To bed.'

'You can't just walk out in the middle of an argument!'

'Yes, I can.'

Jack glared at her in frustration. 'I haven't finished!'

Ellie didn't even look back. 'I think you've said enough,' she said, and walked away down the long corridor to her room.

Jack's jaw worked furiously. He hated the way Ellie did that. He hated the way she just went away rather than face anything she didn't like. She didn't even have the decency to storm and shout back at him. She just left.

He caught up with her at the bedroom door. 'You're going to have to talk to me,' he said angrily. 'We're going to be sleeping in the same bed. You can't just ignore me.'

Ellie turned with her hand on the door. 'I don't think there's any point in us sharing a room, do you, Jack?'

'What about Scott?' Jack was appalled to find himself blustering. 'What's he going to think when he sees us coming out of separate rooms tomorrow morning?'

'It doesn't matter now,' said Ellie, and she closed the door in his face.

She lay awake all night, too numb to cry. Why hadn't she realised how much Jack disliked her? His cruel words echoed endlessly in Ellie's head.

Dull.

Whingeing.

Pathetic.

Ellie burned with shame and humiliation when she remembered how hopefully she had dressed for him that night. She should have known that it would take more than a skirt and a dash of lipstick to change Jack's mind. All she had done was make herself look ridiculous.

Jack was right, she *was* pathetic. It had been pathetic to hope that he would come to love her, pathetic to believe that if he ever looked for another woman after Pippa it would be her, pathetic to waste all those years dreaming about something that could never be.

Well, now the dreaming was over.

Jack was never going to forgive her for not being Pippa; Ellie knew that now. It was time to put an end to a situation that was making them both miserable. They had tried, but their marriage hadn't worked, and she loved him too much to stay and keep on hoping that things would get better. Jack needed a chance to be happy, and he wasn't going to be with her.

The only thing she could do for him now was to go.

CHAPTER TEN

ELLIE was giving Alice her supper the next day when she heard the sound of boots on the verandah and she tensed. She knew that she had to talk to Jack, but she wasn't ready, not yet. She couldn't face him now, when she was numb with misery and exhaustion, and too desperate to explain calmly and clearly why she had to leave him.

They had barely spoken that morning. Jack had left early with Scott and they had been mustering all day. For once, Ellie had been glad not to be out there with the men. She'd needed to be alone to think about what she should do. But in the end she hadn't been able to think about anything but the longing to fall into a deep sleep and wake up to discover that this had all been a bad dream.

'Ellie?'

With a rush of relief, Ellie realised that it was Scott, and not Jack, and she got to her feet, Alice's empty bowl in her hand. 'Back already?' she asked, summoning a smile.

Scott nodded as he came into the kitchen. 'The other guys are bringing the herd in now,' he told her, 'but I need to get back to Mathison before dark, so I came ahead to get my bag and say goodbye to you and Alice.'

Ellie wondered whether to ask Scott not to say anything about the obvious tensions between her and Jack, but in the end it didn't seem to matter that much. Everyone would know soon enough that their marriage was

167

over. 'Thank you for coming,' was all she said instead, as she carried Alice out onto the verandah to see him off.

'No worries.' Scott put his hat on his head and hesitated. 'Are you OK, Ellie?' he asked in concern. 'You don't look too good.'

'I'm fine.' Ellie's voice was tight, her smile brittle. 'Everything's fine.'

Only everything wasn't fine. Numbly, she watched Scott walk away towards the airstrip. He stopped at the junction of the two tracks, and she saw that he had met Jack, coming up from the yards. They stood for a moment, talking, and even from a distance Ellie could see the tension in Jack's lean, rangy figure and the grimness in his expression.

Her heart cracked at the sight of him. It was hard to remember now his lazy good humour or the effortless charm that had been so typical of him. Once he had been carefree and relaxed, once there had been a devastating, daredevil glint in his brown eyes and his smile had been irrepressible. No more. Marriage had turned him into a dour stranger with shuttered eyes and lines of strain in his face. *She* had done that to him.

She saw him lift his hand in unsmiling farewell to Scott, and continue on his way to the homestead. Alice wriggled in her arms. 'Dada!' she said, pointing excitedly.

'I know.' Ellie's throat was unbearably tight as she watched Jack walk towards her and knew that the decision she had made last night was the right one. She would have to go to give him any chance to be happy…but how could she bear to leave him, and Alice? Everything she loved most in the world was here at Waverley Creek. Somehow she was going to have to find the strength to turn and walk away.

Jack halted at the bottom of the steps and looked up at where Ellie stood with Alice in her arms. Her eyes looked enormous in her pale face, and they held an expression of such anguish that his heart stumbled.

'Did you say goodbye to Scott?' he asked, his voice rough with concern.

Ellie couldn't trust herself to speak. She nodded dumbly instead, and Jack hesitated, feeling inadequate to comfort her. He had suspected that she loved Scott—she had practically told him, hadn't she?—but he hadn't realised just how much until now, when he saw in her face what it had cost her to watch the other man leave.

'Are you all right?' he asked gruffly.

Why did they keep asking her that? Of course she wasn't all right! Ellie tried to say that she was fine, as she had said to Scott, but the words wouldn't come out, and to her horror she felt her mouth begin to wobble. She clapped her hand over it to hide its treacherous weakness, and stared back at Jack with appalled green eyes. She never cried. She couldn't cry now. If she let herself cry now, she wouldn't be able to stop.

Without thinking, Jack came quickly up the steps towards her. 'Ellie—' he began, but Ellie couldn't face him any longer. Thrusting Alice into his arms, she pushed past him and stumbled down the steps.

'Ellie!' he cried, but she was running now towards the creek, and with Alice protesting at her undignified transfer into his arms, he could only stare impotently after her.

There was a sick feeling in the pit of his stomach. He had been furious with Ellie the night before. The marriage had been her idea, after all, and it was too late now for her to start complaining about being bored. Her resentment had caught Jack on the raw, and although the anger had continued to churn through him all day when he'd thought about the things that she had said, it had been edged with a peevish sense of guilt. He *hadn't* treated her as a partner, Jack had realised uncomfortably, but that had only made him feel worse.

He had been bracing himself for another stilted evening with Ellie, but the moment he had looked up into her face and seen the naked misery in her eyes all the rage and turmoil inside him had evaporated. He had thought only to comfort her, but Ellie hadn't wanted anything from him. She had run away rather than tell him how she really felt, and Jack was left looking after her with a terrible feeling that he had taken a wrong turn somewhere and lost something precious along the way.

When Ellie finally made her way back from the creek, Jack was bathing Alice. Or rather, he was crouching by the bath, his sleeves rolled up and one hand hovering somewhere behind Alice's back in case she toppled backwards. Alice objected on principle to anyone trying to help her, and insisted on being left to wash herself, which made the whole process not only lengthy but nerve-wracking, at least as far as Jack was concerned.

Ellie was much better at dealing with Alice, Jack acknowledged to himself. By the time he came in she usually had his daughter fed and bathed, and he was left with the easy part. Today, he had had little choice but to carry on with Alice's normal routine as much as possible, and it was proving an uncomfortable lesson not only in how much Ellie did but in how guilty he was of taking her for granted.

He would make it up to her, Jack vowed. He glanced up when Ellie appeared in the doorway, and tried to smile, but she looked so awful that it never quite reached his lips. Her skin was blotched and her eyes red and swollen where she had obviously been crying. Jack's heart twisted. He had never seen Ellie cry before.

Ellie sat down on the edge of the bath and pushed her hair wearily behind her ears. 'I'm sorry about earlier,' she said in a low voice.

'Don't worry about it,' said Jack, shocked by her distress. The look in her eyes reminded him of the way he had felt when Pippa died. Did Ellie feel the same sense of hopeless despair when she had to watch Scott walk away to his nice wife and his life that had nothing to do with her? If she did, she must love him more than Jack had realised. More than he had wanted to realise.

'You were…upset,' he added, trying to show her that he understood.

Ellie looked down at her hands. *Upset.* It seemed a funny word to describe the tearing despair that had been clawing at her ever since she had realised just how peripheral she was to Jack's life. 'I'm just tired, that's all.'

Oblivious to the tensions above her head, Alice was smacking her hands into the water and chortling at the splashes she could make. Jack retrieved the flannel she had discarded earlier and handed it back to her in the hope that she would use it to wash herself, but Alice only threw it back in the water. 'No!' she said firmly.

Sighing, Jack fished it out again. Mindlessly, he wrung it out and wondered how best to help Ellie. At least he could start by apologising. 'I'm sorry about last night,' he said, looking up at her.

'No, it was my fault.' Ellie avoided his eyes. 'We both knew what the situation was when we married. I thought that things would be all right…but they're not, are they, Jack?'

Jack hesitated, then shook his head. There was no point

in trying to pretend that everything was OK. It would only make things more difficult for Ellie. 'No,' he said, 'they're not.'

Ellie took a shuddering breath and willed herself to get through what she had to say next without giving in to tears again. 'Jack, do you remember the agreement we made before we were married?'

Remember it? How could he ever forget it? Jack wondered a little bitterly, but he nodded and waited for her to go on.

'You made me promise that if I ever wanted to leave, I would tell you.' She paused. 'I want to go now, Jack.'

The room seemed to darken around Jack and he stared blindly at Alice. 'Why now?' he asked in a voice that seemed to belong to someone else. 'Nothing's changed.'

'*I've* changed.' Ellie paused, groping for the words to make him understand why she had to leave without telling him the truth that would only make things more difficult than they already were. 'I thought I could bear it, but I can't.'

'We could make some changes,' Jack offered with an edge of desperation. 'I haven't involved you in the running of Waverley the way I should have, I know that, but I'll try harder,' he promised. He couldn't believe that Ellie was sitting there, calmly talking about leaving him. How could he possibly manage without her?

'I'll get a housekeeper,' he hurried on before she could refuse. 'A girl who could help with the cooking and with Alice so that you could spend more time outside, the way you want to. That would make a difference, wouldn't it?'

'Oh, Jack…' Ellie looked at him helplessly. 'I know I complained about being stuck in the homestead, but that's not really the problem.'

'Then what is?'

'It's…the way I feel,' she said inadequately.

There was a desperate silence. Jack lifted a protesting Alice out of the bath and wrapped her in a towel on his knee. He didn't look at Ellie.

'You're still in love with him, aren't you?'

Taken aback by the abruptness of his voice, she stared at him. 'With who?'

Jack couldn't bring himself to say Scott's name. 'You told me you'd always loved someone,' he reminded her in the same harsh tone. 'You said it was hopeless. That was why you were prepared to marry me.'

'Yes.'

'*Are* you still in love with him?'

Ellie looked at Jack. She could draw his face in her sleep. She knew exactly how many lines creased the corners of his eyes, how the hair grew at his temples, the precise length of the tiny scar on his jaw. They were part of her in a way she couldn't explain.

'Yes,' she said.

'And he's the reason you want to go?'

Ellie drew a shaky breath. 'Yes.'

She wished that she could make Jack understand that it was for his sake that she was going. The truth hovered on her tongue, but she couldn't bring herself to say the words. The very thought of the appalled disbelief in his expression if she told him that she loved him made her cringe. It would only make things worse for him. No, better by far to let him believe, as he seemed to, that she loved someone else.

'I thought it would help that neither of us could have what we really wanted,' she went on carefully, 'but it doesn't. It just makes things twice as bad for both of us, and they'll only get worse. I'm never going to be Pippa, Jack. I'm never going to have what I really want either, and I know now that nothing else will do. The longer I stay, the more bitter and resentful we'll both get.'

She glanced at Jack's face, but it was closed and cold. Didn't he understand? Couldn't he *see*?

'I'm sorry,' she finished drearily.

Sorry? What use was sorry? thought Jack bitterly. 'What about Alice?' he said. It was unfair to use Alice as emotional blackmail, but he didn't feel very fair at the moment.

Ellie bit her lip. 'I won't go immediately. Of course I'll wait until you've found someone else to look after her.'

'Thanks.'

The bitter irony in his voice made her wince. 'I'm doing this for you, too, Jack,' she pointed out. 'It'll be better for both of us in the end.'

'And Alice?'

'It'll be better for her, too. It's not good for her to grow up in an unhappy house.'

'It doesn't have to be unhappy,' said Jack stubbornly.

Why was he making it so difficult for her? 'It's what it has been,' said Ellie, her voice cold with the effort of not crying. 'It's what it will be.' She swallowed hard. 'I'm not the right wife for you, Jack. You promised you would let me go if I asked.'

Jack was mechanically drying Alice's toes. 'Yes, I did,' he agreed dully, without looking up. 'Of course you can go, if that's what you want.'

It wasn't what she wanted, but it was what they both needed. Ellie had to remind herself of that again and again over the next ten days. Every nerve in her body screamed at her to throw her pride to the wind, tell Jack the truth and beg him to let her stay after all, but she knew that she couldn't do it.

Better to make a clean break now than to let the situation drag on and on. No matter what Jack said, he would meet someone else eventually, someone he could love the way that he had loved Pippa, and Ellie couldn't bear to be there then. She would be a burden to him, making him feel guilty and resentful for not needing her the way she desperately, desperately needed him.

No, it was better to go now.

Better, but hard. Oh, God, it was hard...

Jack made no attempt to persuade her to change her mind. He treated her with a distant courtesy that hurt Ellie more than his anger had done. He had rung the agency in Darwin the very next day, and asked them to send out a housekeeper as soon as possible.

'They haven't got anyone suitable immediately available,' he'd said when he told Ellie what he had done. 'In the meantime,' he had gone on stonily, 'I suggest we carry on as normal.'

'Of course,' Ellie had said quietly, but how could she behave normally when there was a cold, leaden weight inside her, dragging her down? When it was an effort just to breathe, and she moved slowly and stiffly, like an old woman hunched over her pain?

She did her best. She cooked and she cleaned and she watched Alice grow daily more confident in her steps. She heard her try new words, and her heart splintered to think that the baby would turn into a little girl and she wouldn't be there to see it. Someone else would pick Alice up when she fell and kiss her bruises better. Someone else would cuddle her on their lap and read her a bedtime story, and watch her lashes droop with sleep.

Someone else would water the garden, and cook the

vegetables that she had sown. Someone else would serve the meals and listen to the stockmen as they talked in their slow voices about bull-wrestling and rodeos and what could be done about the dam over at Coollee Bore.

Someone else would sit on the verandah with Jack and watch the stars. She would be gone. She would be far away in the city, learning to live without him all over again.

Every time the phone rang Ellie braced herself for the news that a housekeeper had been found. Every day she dreaded the moment when Jack would tell her that he didn't need her any longer and that she could go. But as day followed day, and nothing happened, she began to long instead for the worst. The waiting, the not knowing when she would have to face saying goodbye, was agony. Terrified that her resolution would fail if she stayed any longer, Ellie prayed that the agency would find someone soon and put her out of her misery.

But when it happened, she was still unprepared. She was peeling potatoes for the evening meal when Jack came into the kitchen.

'I've just been talking to the agency,' he announced without preamble. 'They've found a housekeeper. She's about fifty, but she says she likes children, and she's got good references as a cook.'

Ellie stared down at the potato in her hand. This was the moment she had been preparing herself for, and now it was here and all she wanted to do was to shout that it was too soon, she wasn't ready. There was a cruel, icy grip around her heart, its talons clawing, tearing, squeezing so agonisingly that she had to close her eyes against the pain.

It took a moment for her to be able to speak, and when

she did her voice seemed to belong to someone else. 'She sounds ideal.'

'Her name's Wanda,' said Jack. 'She's worked in the outback before, so she knows what to expect.'

'Good.' Ellie's hands were shaking so much that the peeler kept slipping off the potato. 'When can she come?'

'The day after tomorrow.'

It was too soon, thought Ellie in panic. She swallowed. 'So that will be it.'

'Yes,' said Jack heavily. 'That will be it.'

'I...I can think about going, then.'

Jack tensed. 'You'll stay and meet Wanda, won't you?' he said, clutching at any excuse to keep her longer, but Ellie was already shaking her head.

'I think it would be easier for all of us if I went before she arrives.'

'But that means going tomorrow!'

The weight of despair inside Ellie was so great that she almost buckled beneath it. 'I... Yes... I...I guess it does,' she said unevenly.

She was going.

Jack stared at her as she stood at the sink. Her back was completely familiar to him, he realised, and it would be the last he would see of her the next day when she turned and walked away from him.

He had known that she wanted to go, but it was only now that he understood what it was going to mean. She was going to go, and he would be left here on his own. The homestead would be empty and echoing without her. When he came in she wouldn't be there, moving around the kitchen, carrying Alice on her hip, turning to smile at him. Jack thought of all the times he had taken her warm, quiet presence for granted, and cursed himself for a fool.

Ellie was just standing there, peeling potatoes. She wasn't even looking at him, but for Jack it was as if the world had suddenly shifted around him, spinning everything that was familiar into a pattern that was at once new and dazzlingly clear. Jolted, jarred by the abrupt transformation, he could only stare at her back.

He was in love with her.

It was so obvious, he thought, shocked at his own stupidity. Why hadn't he realised it before? All those weeks he had been fighting it, refusing to acknowledge how much he needed her, and now she was going to go, and it was too late.

'Ellie—' he said urgently, and then stopped.

She turned from the sink, a potato in one hand and the peeler in the other, and something in his expression made her eyes widen. 'What is it?' she asked in concern. 'What's wrong?'

Everything's wrong! Jack wanted to shout. I love you and I'm about to lose you! The temptation to jerk her into his arms and kiss her until she promised to stay was so strong that he had to clench his hands by his sides to stop himself striding over to the sink.

Nothing had changed just because he knew now what he should have known weeks ago, he realised bleakly. He might be in love with her, but Ellie was still in love with Scott. Jack knew that if he begged her she would probably stay, for Alice's sake, but what use was that? He didn't want her to stay because she felt sorry for him. He didn't want her to stay for Alice. He didn't want her to be *kind*.

He wanted her to stay because she loved him, because she needed him the way he needed her. He wanted her desire, not her pity.

And he wanted her to be happy, Jack realised. She was

right; she would never be happy here with him, any more than he would be able to accept being second-best. It was better for her to leave and make a fresh start where she could try and forget Scott, where she wouldn't have to see him or listen to him telling her how happy he was with Anna.

'Jack?'

'Nothing,' he said curtly. 'Nothing's wrong.'

'We should talk.'

It was Jack who broke the silence in the end. They were in the kitchen, washing up the dishes as they always did after an interminable evening meal. They moved carefully around the room in case they touched each other accidentally. They always did that, too.

The chink of crockery was deafening in the strained atmosphere. Ellie kept her head bent and concentrated on washing the pots, scrubbing each one with an obsessive attention to detail.

'I suppose we should,' she muttered as she laid the last saucepan on the drainer.

Jack picked it up and began to dry it. 'If you're leaving tomorrow, we need to sort out a few practicalities,' he said, the tightness in his throat making it hard to keep his voice level. 'I'll pay you for your share of Waverley, of course, but I may not be able to do it immediately. It will take some time to arrange, and in the meantime I'll give you an allowance.'

Mindlessly, Ellie wiped around the sink. 'I don't want any money, Jack,' she said, trying to ignore the pounding behind her eyes. 'I don't want anything.'

'We had an agreement,' he insisted. 'You're my wife and you're legally entitled to my support. You've spent all this time here, looking after Alice, and you haven't got anything out of it.'

Ellie thought of the times she had watched the sun set over Waverley Creek. She thought of seeing Alice take her first steps, of the sound of Jack's boots on the verandah. She had memories that she would treasure for the rest of her life, memories of Jack's lips, of the feel of his body, of the touch of his hand.

'Yes, I have,' she said quietly.

'You'll need some money to start again.' Jack set his jaw stubbornly. 'It's the least I can do for you.' He hesitated. 'Have you told your parents yet?'

Unable to clean anything else, Ellie wrung out the cloth and draped it over the drainer. She hadn't thought about what her family would say. She hadn't been able to think about anything except how she was going to bear leaving him, and Alice, and Waverley Creek.

Wiping her hands on her jeans, she took a steadying breath and turned to face Jack and forced a smile. 'No,' she said. 'Not yet.'

Jack looked at her. There was an air of fragility about her now, as if the slightest blow would shatter her into a thousand pieces, but her head was tilted at a gallant angle and his heart ached at the bravery in her smile.

'What are you going to do, Ellie?' he made himself ask, instead of doing what he wanted to do and putting his arms around her to stop her being hurt ever again. 'Where are you going to go?'

Ellie's careful smile faltered, and her eyes slid desperately away from his. 'I don't know exactly,' she confessed, wishing that she could lie to him, 'but I'll be fine. There's no need to worry about me.'

'But, Ellie—'

All at once Ellie couldn't bear any more. 'I...I'd better

go and pack,' she muttered, desperate to get out of the kitchen before she started to cry.

Jack saw her turn and head for the door. This was what it was going to be like the next day, when she would turn and walk away from him for good. 'Ellie, don't go!' he blurted out before he could stop himself.

The urgency in his voice stopped Ellie at the door, but she didn't turn round. 'I can't talk now,' she admitted in a shaky whisper.

'No... I mean...don't go, ever,' said Jack desperately. 'Don't go now, don't go tomorrow. Don't ever go.'

Ellie stayed very still, eyes squeezed shut, afraid that he was going to ask her to stay for Alice's sake, terrified that she wouldn't have the strength to refuse.

'Please, Ellie.' Jack walked over to stand behind her, but although his hand went out he let it fall again without touching her. 'Please stay,' he said, no longer caring that he was pleading with her. He didn't care if she stayed out of pity. The only thing that mattered was the knowledge that he couldn't bear her to go and leave him alone.

'I know you want to go,' he said. 'I know I ought to let you go. I thought that I could, but I can't. I didn't mean to say anything,' he stumbled on, 'but when you turned and walked away just now, I knew I couldn't cope without you.'

'You'll find someone else,' said Ellie with difficulty. 'Alice will be fine.'

'*I* won't be.' Jack hesitated, struggling to find the right words. 'I need you, Ellie.'

'It...it's not as if we'll never see each other again,' she managed to say. 'We'll always be friends.'

'I don't want to be friends!' Jack's voice rose to a shout and he stopped, forcing himself to sound calmer. 'Being friends isn't enough.'

There was a moment of intense silence while his words seemed to echo around the kitchen, and then, very slowly, Ellie turned round. Her eyes were green and enormous in her white face, and their expression of disbelief made Jack's sudden rage evaporate. If he hadn't felt so desperate he would have smiled at her shock. How could she not have known?

'I'm in love with you,' he told her, quite simply after all.

Ellie stared at him, unable to move or to speak or to let herself believe what she had heard.

'I know you don't feel the same,' Jack hurried on before she could recover enough to tell him it was hopeless. 'I know you're in love with someone else, and that I haven't done anything to make you love me instead.' His smile twisted. 'I just took you for granted. I let you do everything for me. I let you make my house a home, and care for my daughter, and work until you were ready to drop, and never once did I do anything for you.

'I never showed you how much you mean to me,' he went on more slowly. 'How could I when I didn't know myself? It wasn't until you said that you were going that I realised how empty my life would be without you.'

Ellie swallowed. She felt very strange, almost disorientated, as if this were just a terrible, wonderful dream. 'But…but you love Pippa,' she stammered, surprised to find that she could get the words out at all.

'Yes, I did love her,' said Jack. 'But I didn't love her the way I love you. Pippa was fun and exciting. What we had was wonderful, but somehow never quite real.' He realised it for the first time. 'Perhaps if it had been that stupid argument we had wouldn't have been enough to make her leave, and everything would have been different.'

He sighed. 'I don't know if the love we had would have lasted. Now, it seems like a dream. All I know is that what I feel for you *is* real.'

Still he made no move to touch her, sensing that she was not yet ready to accept what he was saying. 'I wasn't expecting to fall in love with you, Ellie. I don't even know how it happened. You were so close that I couldn't see you for a long time, and then one day I looked and there you were, part of my life, as necessary to me as breathing.

'I'd got used to thinking of you as a friend, but that night we made love it was like coming home. I knew then that I didn't want you as a friend; I wanted you as a lover. I wanted you to belong to me and no one else. I wanted to punch Scott every time he so much as looked at you.'

Jack paused, and when Ellie still didn't say anything he went on quietly, 'I don't deserve another chance, Ellie, but I'll go down on my knees and beg if you'll just say that you'll stay—not for Alice, not because you love Waverley, but because you want to be with me.'

It was a dream. It had to be a dream. Ellie shook her head to clear it, and Jack took an urgent step closer. 'Don't say no!' he pleaded. 'At least think about it! I know you love Scott, but he's got Anna. He doesn't need you, and I do.'

'Scott?' said Ellie in a peculiar voice. 'You think I'm in love with Scott?'

It was Jack's turn to stare. 'You mean you're not?'

'No.'

He had been so sure it was Scott. Now he had to struggle to readjust all his ideas. 'You're in love with someone else?' he said carefully.

She nodded, a smile trembling on her lips.

Jack's first surge of relief at discovering that it wasn't Scott evaporated. What if it was someone who wasn't married, who might just look at Ellie one day and suddenly realise, as he had done, just how beautiful she was?

'You said you'd never have a future with him,' he reminded her. 'Why not stay here with me instead? I'll make you happy,' he promised. 'I'll spend the rest of my life helping you to forget him.'

Ellie found her voice at last. 'I'll never be able to do that, Jack,' she said with a wavering smile.

'You could try, couldn't you? You could learn to love again.' There was a note of desperation in Jack's voice. 'You could change your mind!'

'No, I won't.' Ellie's smile shimmered through her tears. 'He's the only man I'll ever love.'

Her eyes were luminous with love, and Jack turned away, sick at heart that it wasn't for him. Well, he had tried. He had begged her to stay, but it wasn't any good. He should have known that she wouldn't change her mind. Ellie would always be true. She was a one-man woman. He just hoped that the man she loved knew just how lucky he was.

'I see,' he said heavily. Leaning his arms on the table, he stood with his head bowed as he tried to master the bitterness of disappointment. 'Well,' he managed with difficulty, 'that's that, then. You'd better get on with your packing.'

He sensed Ellie's warmth beside him before he felt her hand on his shoulder, and he averted his face, unable to bear the pity he knew would be in her eyes. 'Just go,' he muttered.

'Jack,' she said softly. 'Jack, it's you.'

Jack didn't know what she was talking about. He rubbed his face tiredly. 'What?'

'Look at me, Jack.'

Lifting his head, he stared at her uncomprehendingly.

'It's you,' said Ellie again with an unsteady smile. Her hand slid from his shoulder down to his elbow, curling round to drift lovingly down the inside of his bare forearm and lace her fingers with his. 'It's only ever been you.'

'Me?'

'I've loved you all my life, Jack,' she said simply. 'I could never love anyone else.'

Hope warred with disbelief in his brown eyes. 'You love me?' he asked incredulously, and she smiled tenderly, hardly able to believe herself that she could tell the truth at last.

'I always have. I always will.'

Jack's grip on her hand tightened convulsively. 'Say that again,' he demanded, and pulled her against him so that he could bury his face in her hair. 'Oh, God, Ellie, say it again.'

'I love you, Jack,' she said, her voice breaking as the tears spilled over.

Tangling his fingers in the soft brown hair, he tilted her face up to his. 'Again,' he insisted.

Half-laughing, half-crying, Ellie told him what he wanted to hear. 'I love you, I love you!'

He kissed her then, his lips coming down on hers hungrily. They kissed with a kind of desperation born of the knowledge of how close they had come to losing each other. Ellie put her arms around his neck and gave herself up to the enchantment spilling through her in a golden rush of joy as she began to believe that he loved her as she loved him.

'Why didn't you tell me?' Jack asked breathlessly at

last, kissing her eyes, her cheeks, her nose, her mouth once more.

'I couldn't. I was so sure that you would never love anyone but Pippa. Whenever you talked about her she sounded so wonderful, and so different from me, that it seemed impossible that you could ever look at anyone else. I knew that I could never rival Pippa's ghost, and I thought that if you knew how much I loved you, you would be embarrassed and it would spoil everything. I told myself that it was enough to be married to you, just to be near you. That was all I'd ever wanted.'

Jack lifted his head to look down into her eyes. 'Then why were you going to leave?' he asked, holding her face between his hands and running a thumb along her cheekbone in a tender caress that made Ellie shiver with pleasure.

'Because in the end being near you wasn't enough. It was fine at first, but the more I was with you, the more I loved you, and the more it hurt that you didn't love me back.'

'And I was so jealous of Scott!' Jack shook his head at his own stupidity, and then he smiled, the old, brilliant smile that Ellie had loved for so many years. 'You mean I've spent all this time being jealous of myself?'

Ellie laughed and buried her face in his throat, succumbing to the sheer joy of being able to kiss him and hold him. She clung to him, shivering with pleasure as his arms tightened around her. It was a dream, a wonderful, glorious dream, a happiness so intense that it hardly seemed real.

'I thought it was obvious how much I loved you,' she told him. 'I couldn't believe that you would ever come to love me back.' Drawing back slightly, she looked up into the brown eyes that were warm with love. 'I still can't believe it,' she confessed. 'Not really.'

Jack smiled as he drew her out of the kitchen. 'Then I'll just have to prove it to you,' he said.

'Now do you believe me?'

Ellie stirred at the honeyed pleasure of Jack's hands moving with warm possession over her body. Jack was leaning over her, looking down into her face with an expression of such tenderness that her heart melted with love.

'I believe you.' She wound her arms around his neck and pulled him down for a long, sweet kiss. 'That's not to say that I won't need regular reminders, though!'

'There's no time for that,' said Jack with mock sternness. 'We've got work to do!'

'Yes.' Ellie stretched blissfully at the thought. 'We'd better ring the agency in the morning and tell them that we don't need a housekeeper any more.'

Jack twisted her hair around his finger. 'I've got a better idea,' he said. 'We'll have her here to help in the homestead, and that will give you more time to work outside with me. We've got a lot to do still, Ellie, but this time we'll do it together,' he promised.

Ellie sighed happily. 'This time we'll do it right.'

PARENTS WANTED

Families in the making!

In the orphanage of a small Australian town called Bay Beach are little children desperately in need of love, and dreaming of their very own family....

The answer to their dreams can also be found in Bay Beach! Couples who are destined for each other—even if they don't know it yet. Brought together by love for these tiny children, can they find true love themselves—and finally become a real family?

Titles in this series by fan-favorite **MARION LENNOX** are

A Child in Need—(April HR #3650)
Their Baby Bargain—(July HR #3662)

Look out for further Parents Wanted stories in Harlequin Romance®, coming soon!

Available wherever Harlequin Books are sold.

HARLEQUIN®
Makes any time special ®

NEARLYWEDS

Almost at the altar—will these *nearly*weds become *newly*weds?

Harlequin Romance® is delighted to invite you to some special weddings! Yet these are no ordinary weddings. Our beautiful brides and gorgeous grooms only *nearly* make it to the altar—before fate intervenes.

But the story doesn't end there.... Find out what happens in these tantalizingly emotional novels!

Authors to look out for include:

Leigh Michaels—The Bridal Swap
Liz Fielding—His Runaway Bride
Janelle Denison—The Wedding Secret
Renee Roszel—Finally a Groom
Caroline Anderson—The Impetuous Bride

Available wherever Harlequin books are sold.

HARLEQUIN®
Makes any time special™

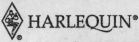

HARLEQUIN®

makes any time special—online...

eHARLEQUIN.com

your romantic life

━Romance 101━━━━━
♥ Guides to romance, dating and flirting.

━Dr. Romance ━━━━
♥ Get romance advice and tips from
our expert, Dr. Romance.

━Recipes for Romance━
♥ How to plan romantic meals for you
and your sweetie.

━Daily Love Dose━━
♥ Tips on how to keep the romance
alive every day.

━Tales from the Heart━
♥ Discuss romantic dilemmas with other
members in our Tales from the Heart
message board.

What happens when you suddenly discover your happy twosome is about to turn into a...*family*?
Do you laugh?
Do you cry?
Or...do you get married?

The answer is all of the above—and plenty more!

Share the laughter and tears with
Harlequin Romance® as these
unsuspecting couples have to be

READY FOR BABY

When parenthood takes you by surprise!

Authors to look out for include:

Caroline Anderson—DELIVERED: ONE FAMILY
Barbara McMahon—TEMPORARY FATHER
Grace Green—TWINS INCLUDED!
Liz Fielding—THE BACHELOR'S BABY

Available wherever Harlequin books are sold.

HARLEQUIN®
Makes any time special ™

True Highland Spirit

by Amanda Forester

Seduction is a powerful weapon...

Morrigan McNab is a Highland lady, robbed of her birthright and with no choice but to fight alongside her brothers to protect their impoverished clan. When she encounters Sir Jacques Dragonet, she discovers her fiercest opponent...

Sir Jacques Dragonet is a Noble Knight of the Hospitaller Order, willing to give his life to defend Scotland from the English. He can't stop himself from admiring the beautiful Highland lass who wields her weapons as well as he can and endangers his heart even more than his life...

Now they're racing each other to find a priceless relic. No matter who wins this heated rivalry, both will lose unless they can find a way to share the spoils.

"A masterful storyteller, Amanda Forester brings new excitement to Scottish medieval romance!"—Gerri Russell, award-winning author of *To Tempt a Knight*

For more Amanda Forester books, visit:

About the Author

Mary Wine was already a multipublished author in romantic suspense, fantasy, and Western romance when her interest in historical reenactment and costuming inspired her to turn her pen to historical romance. She lives with her husband and sons in Southern California, where the whole family enjoys participating in historical reenactment.